D1525608

ONE BAD APPLE

The ONCE UPON A WESTERN Series
by Rachel Kovaciny

BOOKS

Cloaked

Dancing and Doughnuts

One Bad Apple

SHORT STORIES

"No Match for a Good Story"

"Blizzard at Three Bears Lake"

"Gruff"

"Let Down Your Hair"

ONE

BAD

APPLE

Rachel Kovaciny

White Rook Press

Woodbridge, Virginia

This novel is a work of fiction. Names, characters, dialogs, and incidents are the products of the author's imagination and are not to be misconstrued as real. Any resemblance to actual events or people, living or dead, is purely coincidental.

Book design by Rachel Kovaciny
Cover design and illustration by Erika Ohlendorf

White Rook Press, Woodbridge, Virginia, USA.

ISBN-10: 8665454344
ISBN-13: 979-8665454344

For Larry and our kids, with love and devotion.

For Deborah, who sees better from a distance.

In honor of Sidney Poitier.

Soli Deo gloria.

AUTHOR'S NOTE

America's Old West of the 1800s was a very diverse place. Americans of every skin tone contributed to the building of this great nation, but western fiction and films have not always reflected this fact. In this book series, I am attempting to highlight that real-life diversity in a way that stays true to history while presenting fictional stories. *One Bad Apple* has the most diverse cast in the series so far, as the majority of the characters in this book are Black.

I have not attempted to recreate any specific speech patterns, accents, or dialects for my characters. I knew that it would be impossible for me to write dialog that accurately represents dialects spoken by characters who grew up in such diverse places as New Orleans, Ohio, Illinois, and Tennessee.

I consulted with sensitivity readers while creating this book. They shared their invaluable knowledge and understanding with me, and I thank them for that. I strove to present Black characters in a way that is accurate to the history of America and also sensitive toward today's readers. Any inaccurate or insensitive writing that may remain is my own mistake and not theirs.

If you are interested in learning more about Black Americans in the Old West, I have included a list of suggested titles at the back of this book that will give you some ideas for where to start learning more about their contributions to American history.

I have tried to use language that would be accurate to the time period but not be harshly offensive to modern readers. Please be aware that some archaic terms used by characters in this book are not words we should use ourselves today.

--Rachel Kovaciny
July, 2020

CHAPTER ONE

"He's the one." Mrs. Mallone pointed a slender brown finger at me. "Take him away. He did this. He took my husband from me." She seemed to choke on the words. "And my daughter."

"She was your *stepdaughter*," I corrected her. No one heard me over the clamor raised by all those around us. Everyone either burst out weeping afresh or discussed Mrs. Mallone's words and what they should do about them. About me.

My sisters and little cousins huddled in shocked silence near me, away from the mourners, at the edge of the camp. As if they were somehow guilty too, because they happened to be related to me.

Me, the orphan boy about to get hauled away for the deaths of a righteous old man and the kindest girl who ever walked these trails to the west.

Where was Jacob? I looked around, trying to see

1

beyond the edges of the crowd. Where could he be?

Sanderson stepped toward me, away from Mrs. Mallone. "I'll see he gets what he deserves. Don't you worry."

Mrs. Mallone gave herself over to her grieving and sank down on the ground, her anguish louder than the rest. She was the widow, after all. Only right she should cry the loudest. Folks would expect it.

Sanderson pulled my arms behind my back and slid a coil of rope over my right hand.

"I didn't do this." I swiveled my head around so I could see him. "It's all a mistake!" A new fear gripped my fourteen-year-old mind tighter than Sanderson could ever bind my hands. What if he took me away too soon? Before the burying?

"I didn't do this!" I screamed so loudly that the gathered people looked my way. They'd heard me even over all that mournful noise.

All the faces I could see were varying shades of brown. Some so light you could almost call them white, and some so dark they did look truly black by comparison. But the only white faces there were mine and Sanderson's. And my sisters' and cousins', of course.

Sanderson looped the rope around my left hand and yanked it so tight it bit into my wrists and threw me off balance, making me stumble backward.

My sisters began crying when they realized I was about to be dragged off to jail, and my little cousins joined them. Why were my own eyes dry? Seemed like everyone I knew was crying, all except me and Jacob. Where was Jacob?

I wondered how long it would take Sanderson to finish tying my hands. If he would haul me away to jail right then and there. Or did he intend to take me out of earshot and rid this earth of me?

The idea of dying didn't scare me as much as the thought of missing the burying. I just had to be there for it. Otherwise, though the truth would come out clear and loud without me, it would do me no good at all.

Men stood knee-deep in the graves, still digging. Two graves, with about a hundred colored people clustered around them. And us.

Why did graves always come in pairs? First both my parents, years ago, then my aunt and uncle last week, and now Hopeful and her father. Only a week between funerals, I realized with a shiver. Two graves ended this story, just as two graves had begun it.

But we'd had to dig those first ones ourselves.

CHAPTER TWO

A week earlier, we'd had the second grave about half dug when we heard the hoofbeats. Sounded like one horse coming steady up the trail.

Jacob didn't pause swinging his shovel. I didn't know if he'd heard, so I said, "Somebody's coming."

"That's so." He stopped digging to push his dark blond hair out of his eyes with the back of a grimy hand. "You tired?" He figured he was in charge now, being oldest by two years. This was his way of telling me to get a move on.

"No, not very." I set to work again.

I only got a few more shovelfuls of dirt out before the rider finally rounded the bend. I squinted against the late-morning sunlight, trying to make him out. A lean man, I saw, at ease in the saddle. He pulled up when he saw us but didn't call out. Just sat on his big bay horse, hat brim so low it darkened his face with its shadow.

I stopped shoveling. "Maybe he'll help."

Jacob didn't answer.

I'd grown used to that. Even before my aunt and uncle took sick, Jacob hadn't had much use for me. He was nearly sixteen-and-a-half, and I had barely turned fourteen. I'd hoped for years that he'd see me as, if not an equal, at least a person worth passing the time of day with. After all, we had a lot in common: both the oldest child in our family and both boys.

And now, both orphans.

Looking back now that I'm an adult, I can see why he might have avoided me. Taking me and my sisters in when our own folks died a couple years earlier hadn't exactly made life easier for Jacob or his siblings. But at the time, I had wrapped myself up in my own grief too much to realize that. I only knew Jacob had little use for me. Once I gave up trying to be his pal, I stayed out of his way. We barely spoke even on good days.

And that day, digging graves for Jacob's parents and baby brother, was not a good day.

The man nudged his horse forward, slow and cautious. Since Jacob kept on shoveling, I figured it was up to me to talk with this stranger. I clambered out of the grave, one hand shading my eyes so I could see him better. It wasn't until I got a whole lot closer that I realized it wasn't a shadow darkening his face.

I stopped. I'd never spoken to a colored person before. Never even seen one. And now here came a colored man getting closer every second.

My pleas for help stuck to my tongue. I could only stare.

He reined in again. "You folks have had some trouble." He had a deep voice with a drawl that stretched out the midsection of that last word.

"We did. We're still having it."

"What kind?" He didn't look old, maybe ten years older than me. Still, he was an adult, and I figured we needed a grown person's help right about then.

I realized I was staring. My ma and pa would have scolded me for such bad manners. "Fever. My uncle and aunt—they died. And their baby, Andrew."

"Anyone else sick?"

"Not any more. My sister Lillie felt poorly for a few days, but she's better now."

"What about your folks?"

"Got no folks left," I answered. "We'd been living with my aunt and uncle back in Illinois. Going west to Kansas to get us a bigger farm."

"And now?"

"Now we're burying them."

"I meant after that. You got any other kin?"

"We got another uncle in Kansas already. We

were supposed to meet up with him. Him and Uncle Drew were all set to stake claims together and build a big farm with room for all of us."

"How many of you are there?"

"Seven now, counting me."

"How come you're out here alone?"

"When the fever struck, the wagon train wouldn't wait with us. Said we could stay here until Uncle Drew and Aunt Phoebe got well. Said another train would come along and we could join it."

"But they didn't get well."

"No. And now we're burying them and waiting for another train. Are you with a wagon train?"

"I am." He eyed the two graves where Jacob still toiled. Then he looked back at the trail. With a sigh, he swung down from his horse. "We'd best get your burying finished. Then we'll see what's to be done with you. What's your name?"

"Levi Dalton. That's my cousin, Jacob."

"Where're the others?"

"Laura and Martha took the little ones out to the creek to water our horses and play." I pointed at the dip in the distance where scrubby trees marked a shallow stream.

We had almost reached the graveside. It occurred to me that I didn't know this dark stranger's name, though he'd been polite and asked mine. "What's your name?" I looked up at him, my eyes not tired yet of the wonder of his skin, so different from any I'd ever seen.

"Ness." He held out his left hand.

I'm ashamed now to admit it, but I thought maybe colored folks shook hands the opposite way of white folks. That's how little I knew. I expected them to somehow *be* different, not only look different. Not wanting to seem ignorant myself, I shook with my own left. His palm looked pink compared with the back of his hand, not much different from mine where we touched.

Ness snorted a half-laugh. "You have some good manners, Levi Dalton. Now lend me your shovel. Graves don't dig themselves."

My ears heated up, and I knew they gave away my embarrassment. "Sorry. Thank you. Here." I held out the shovel.

Ness took it and passed me his horse's reins. "Take her for a drink?"

"Sure." Glad for something to do besides dig, I led the big bay mare away almost cheerfully. Sometimes I forgot for a minute that my aunt and uncle had passed on, and baby Andrew. I'd learned that trick when my own folks died, one not three months after the other. It made breathing easier, sometimes, not to be always remembering sorrow. Didn't help my sleeping, though.

I glanced back in time to see Ness drop down in

the grave and catch Jacob's rhythm, swinging his own shovel with relentless strokes. Jacob didn't even look at him, just kept moving that dirt.

Walking to the creek, I remembered my pa's burying, and my ma's. Both were two years gone by then, and the sights and sounds of their funerals had dulled some. The ache of missing them had become a tender throb and not the first sharp pain I'd thought would split me like kindling. But we hadn't had to dig their graves. We'd had neighbors who dug the first hole in the churchyard, and then another a few months later, when Ma faded out of this life from missing Pa.

I'd been glad to dig alongside Jacob, but I was gladder still that this man Ness had offered his help. I was used to hoeing, chopping wood, and such, but my palms had burned from shifting that shovel. I examined them, for focusing on my blisters was easier than considering the fresh hurt in my heart.

Uncle Drew and Aunt Phoebe had been kindness itself to me, Laura, and Lillie. They never once complained about the way we overflowed their house and stretched their food thin. Simply pulled us close and made us know we still had folks that loved us.

Now, grown man that I am, I feel ashamed that I never showed more gratitude for their kindness. As a boy, though, it had seemed natural that they would take us in. It wasn't until I lost them too that I learned not everyone thinks orphans are owed whatever help anyone can give them.

I stumbled over a rock, the jolt knocking loose the tears waiting behind my eyes. I hated the thought of leaving them behind us on this empty bit of scrubby Missouri land. I swiped my eyes with my sleeve. Fourteen years old and crying—wouldn't do to let anyone see. I was the man of my family now, protector of my sisters, even if Jacob had decided he could take charge of us all. I had to be done with crying.

By the time I reached the creek, my eyes were dry again.

"Whose horse is that?" my sister Laura asked. She'd been sitting on a half-rotten log, plaiting her long brown hair, but she got up when she saw me.

"A man named Ness. He's helping Jacob." I let the horse lower its head and drink. Laura and our cousin Martha had staked our two teams and Uncle Drew's riding horse out in a patch of grass so they could graze.

The younger children waded in the stream, my youngest sister Lillie holding her skirt high and staying away from our cousins Henry and Caleb in case they splashed her. She was ten and growing as particular as twelve-year-old Laura. Not that Henry and Caleb were doing much splashing. They were old enough to understand the solemnity of our new situation. Somewhat, anyhow.

Laura reached out and patted the bay's neck. "Is he with a wagon train?"

"He said so. Must be a scout." Our train had had two men who worked for the wagon master as scouts. They rode ahead each day to find any possible obstacles and hindrances, good places to stop for the night, and such.

Eleven-year-old Martha looked my way, but she didn't join our conversation. She'd not spoken since we woke that morning and found her parents had forsaken us sometime in the night, along with her baby brother.

Lillie waded over to us. "Think they'll let us join them?"

"What else can they do?" I fingered the leather reins I held. "He's a colored man."

"What?" my sisters exclaimed together.

"It's true. Skin as dark as fresh-turned earth." I couldn't resist adding, "He shook my hand." I neglected mentioning that it had been a backwards, accidental-like handshake.

Even that didn't get Martha to speak. She was too numb. I knew. I remembered. Martha was lost in a fog where nothing could touch her. I missed that fog sometimes. The day would come when she'd lose that and feel it all, too much and all the time. I remembered.

Ness's bay mare finished drinking. She snorted, blowing water drops in every direction, particularly mine. I wiped my face again, grateful for a reason for a wet sleeve, should anyone notice. Not that anyone would. We had a funeral to conduct. Tears would be expected there. I could do any leftover crying then.

CHAPTER THREE

When we returned from the stream, Jacob and Ness had the second grave finished.

Ness didn't need us to ask him for help with what came next. He climbed in the wagon bed where me and Laura and Martha had wrapped the bodies in the oldest sheets we had.

Ness helped me and Jacob carry Uncle Drew and Aunt Phoebe and lower them into their last resting places. We'd figured we'd put baby Andrew with Aunt Phoebe. Didn't seem right to put him in the ground by himself.

Martha carried Andrew, not letting anyone else hold him. While she silently rocked his little body wrapped in a pillowcase, I moved closer to Ness. "Do you know the words for a burying?"

"Not rightly. But they've got a preacher in the wagon train. A real minister, been to school and all.

He's a good man. They should reach here before nightfall. I know he'd be willing to give your family a proper funeral."

"A proper funeral would be nice."

"I got to ride back now. Let them know about you. See what's to be done."

"Should we cover them up now?"

"It'd be best. Funeral prayers will mean the same whether the dirt's over them already or not."

I didn't relish the thought of using that shovel again so soon. Still, we'd have something to keep us busy until the wagon train arrived, real minister and all.

We heard them long before we saw them. The pounding of hundreds of hooves, the creaking of wagons, and the squeak of leather harnesses—those sounds had filled our lives since we left St. Louis. I can still close my eyes and hear them as though this happened yesterday, not years ago.

Three weeks we'd been traveling before the fever struck, bumping and jolting over those roads used by thousands before us as they aimed their own wagons for Independence. We followed the hoofprints and wheel ruts of the pioneers who'd crossed to Oregon and California and such. Places I'd heard about all my life. Promised Lands of a sort.

Jacob stabbed three rude crosses down in the dirt, two at the head of one grave and one at the head of the other. They were nothing more than broken branches tied together with stringy weeds, but they were the best we could do. "Should have names," Jacob said angrily as if it was someone's fault the crosses had no names. "Should be made of stone. Should be proper."

"At least the funeral will be proper," I offered.

"At least." He wrung so much scorn out of those two words, I resolved not to speak to him again until after the funeral.

I turned my back on Jacob and watched the wagons. Ness rode close to the lead wagon, speaking with its driver, a woman. They gestured broadly at each other, and I suspected them of disagreeing. But finally, the team of horses slowed and turned off the road, and I could see the driver was colored too.

A young woman ran up to the lead wagon. She reached up and undid the back of the wagon so it folded down on a hinge like a sideways door. After pulling out a set of wooden steps and settling them beneath, she helped an older man down, holding his hand for steadiness. Like Ness and the wagon's driver, their skin was black.

The older man tucked the younger woman's hand into the crook of his arm. The big leather-covered book he carried must be his Bible. This would be the preacher, then.

Ness spoke with the woman driving, and she slapped the reins on the backs of her horses and ordered them to get up, now. She aimed her team back toward the road, but in a curve, and the other wagons swung in a loose circle. It appeared they meant to make camp nearby. I felt honored that strangers would stop their journey so the preacher could pray over our dead.

I had the sudden realization that I had gone from never seeing one single colored person in my life to seeing four up close in one day. Life's changes come all in a rush like that sometimes, going from drought to downpour in a breath. I learned that young.

Ness dismounted and made introductions. "This here's the Reverend Eli Mallone," Ness said, slow and stately. "And his daughter, Miss Hopeful," he added. His lips quirked, ready to smile but knowing now was not the time.

The Reverend Eli Mallone took off his hat and revealed snowy hair cropped close to his head. "I'm grieved for your loss. And I'm thankful to the Lord we happened by in your hour of need." He had a kind of musical voice, his words sounding like a song he might sing any moment. They had a rhythm to them, is what I mean. Same as the Psalms or poetry. Maybe that came of being a preacher. His skin was darker than Ness's, his face creased with fine wrinkles around the mouth and eyes. Dark spots dotted his cheeks below his eyes.

I speculated about his age. He must be older than my aunt and uncle, surely, but if the young woman was his daughter, he could not be so awfully old. And yet, he walked with a hesitancy, almost a shuffle, that made me think of the oldest people I'd known back home, old ladies who sat beside the fire and kept babies from falling into the flames while the young mothers did chores.

Jacob said, "If someone had happened by a day or two ago, we wouldn't be in need. Someone with medicine to help would've been more of a blessing. Or would you say the Lord works in mysterious ways, and my ma and pa and baby brother dying is part of a plan." He stuck his chin out, defiant, angry.

"Jacob!" I protested. If Jacob's spiteful sassing offended the preacher, might he not turn around and go back without speaking any words of comfort and peace to us? I found myself craving those words I'd heard twice before about those I'd loved. Not so much the part about ashes and dust as the part about that sure and certain hope.

The Reverend Eli only nodded. "I could say that. Would it help you if I did?"

Jacob glared at him.

"Well, if it won't help, then I won't bother saying such." He released his daughter's hand from his arm

17

and stepped in front of the graves beside the three crooked crosses. He motioned for us to gather close, and Ness and Hopeful stood on either side of him. When Ness took his hat off, Jacob and I did the same, and we all waited.

The Reverend Eli looked up at the sky and closed his eyes. "Lord Jesus," he prayed, "you know all and you love all. You know the pain these children of yours feel. Why, you yourself cried when those you loved had died. You promised to preserve our going out and our coming in, whether it be journeys here on earth or the last journey to our eternal home.

"You tell us that your thoughts are not our thoughts, and we know not why you have allowed these believers to fall asleep in you, leaving behind those who mourn. We have no fear for those who have gone home to you, but those who remain seek to understand your will for them.

"Bless and protect these children as they find their way now without the parents you gave them. Without the baby brother they loved and took joy in. Strengthen and preserve them on their way, Lord Jesus. Give them comfort and peace. The comfort and peace they can find only in you. Give them guidance and protection and bring them safely to whatever new home you have already prepared for them, be it in this life or the next. Amen."

Ness and Hopeful chorused, "Amen."

Beside me, Laura slipped her hand into mine. I found, standing beside those two new mounds, that my tears had all deserted me. I felt numb and weary. Breathing was all the movement I could manage.

And then a low, clear voice sang, *Amazing grace, how sweet the sound that saved a wretch like me.* It was the Reverend Eli's daughter, Hopeful.

I marveled at her voice, so quiet and sweet, and yet not weak or bashful. It matched her kind, pretty face with a pointed chin and large eyes. She wore her thick black hair pulled back in a modest knot at the base of her neck. Her dress was plain and gray, covered with an apron stained a weary brown from day after day of walking in the dirt kicked up by the wagon train's animals. But her pure voice lit her from within, and I believed for a moment that she was the most beautiful girl I would ever see.

The Reverend Eli joined his daughter on the next line, his voice as deep and melodious in song as I had expected. *I once was lost, but now am found; was blind, but now I see.*

I looked around at my sisters and cousins. We knew this hymn too. I took a deep breath and added my voice to theirs, though it had become prone to breaking of late. *Through many dangers, toils, and snares I am already come.*

Laura squeezed my hand. She and Lillie sang with us, *His grace has brought me safe thus far, and grace will lead me home.*

Jacob's face had stiffened, his mouth a grim slit. Had I looked that way at my pa's funeral, or my ma's? Likely, I had.

Ness joined in next. *The Lord has promised good to me. His word my hope secures.*

Henry and Caleb added their high, childish voices to the song, and I envied how their voices never cracked the way mine did. *He will my shield and portion be as long as life endures.*

Beyond my sisters, I heard Martha begin singing too. *Yes, when this flesh and heart shall fail and mortal life shall cease, I shall possess within the veil a life of joy and peace.*

I kept watching Jacob. When Martha began singing—Martha, who had not spoken a word all day—he opened his lips in surprise, though he did not sing with us.

Those were all the verses I knew. But Ness, Hopeful, and the Reverend Eli continued, singing one more I'd not heard before. Their three voices swelled until they sounded louder than when we'd all sung together. *When we've been there ten thousand years, bright shining as the sun, we've no less days to sing God's praise than when we'd first begun.*

There came the lump in my throat that I'd expected all along. A tear or two slipped down my cheeks, and I swiped them away with my free hand.

The Reverend Eli looked up at the sky again. "Lord Jesus, you remind us that we brought nothing into this world, and it is sure and certain we can take nothing out of it. We cometh up only to be cut down like a flower and, in the very midst of life, we are in death. But like a father pitieth his own children, so you, Lord Jesus, pity those of us who love and fear you.

"Now we commend into your hands these dear ones, even as we commit their bodies to the ground, in the sure and certain hope of the resurrection unto eternal life that is ours through you, our dear Lord Jesus. Ashes to ashes, and dust to dust, for dust we are, and to dust we shall return. Amen."

Dutifully, we all chorused, "Amen."

And that was that. Like a gear wheel lurching to the next cog, life slipped from old to new. From that moment, we left behind Uncle Drew and Aunt Phoebe and the life they had provided for us, and we moved forward into what would become our new life without them. Though we still stood around their graves, we were somehow pushing and slipping away already.

CHAPTER FOUR

The Reverend Eli stayed beside the graves for some time, his eyes closed in prayer. His daughter Hopeful walked around to us. "Can you tell me your names?" she asked kindly, kneeling down to look at Henry and Caleb more on a level.

The little ones turned away, all shy. Martha stared at her, but didn't speak. Laura named us all off and gave our ages. On the other side of the graves, Jacob and Ness argued. Ness gestured toward our wagons. Jacob pointed at the circled wagon train. Since I was now the head of my part of the family, I decided I had a right to listen in on any planning Jacob might be doing, even if he deemed my agreement unneeded. I made my way around the graves so I could at least hear them.

I arrived in time to hear Ness say, "You don't know that."

"It's been near onto a week since our train left us here. You're the first to show," Jacob disagreed. "No telling how long before the next people come by. We can't sit here and wait."

"This uncle of yours you're going to meet—you have any way of contacting him?"

"He's to meet us in Junction City, is all I know."

"You could try to wire him there."

"Wire him from where?"

"We passed a town two days back. One of us could take you back there."

"My uncle can't come get us. He's staked his claim already, and he's got to live there and prove up on it."

"He could send for you."

Jacob insisted, "We'll waste weeks, maybe, and then have to keep on heading west anyway."

"You could always sell your wagons and buy train tickets. There's a train goes to Junction City."

I sighed. This man Ness had no idea how stubborn Jacob could be. The surest way of making him refuse to do something was by urging him to do it. Me, I thought taking a train to Kansas sounded real sensible. But I could see there was no use in saying so.

"No," Jacob argued, "we need these wagons and tools for our new farms. That's why we're bringing them. Otherwise, we could've all ridden the train.

But my folks... we saved and collected this up on purpose. We got my ma's dishes and my pa's tools— they're what we have left to remember them by. And our horses, and our clothes, and our food..." Jacob's voice rose, louder and higher.

While my cousin spoke, Hopeful Mallone stepped up beside me. She stood no taller than myself, though I judged she was older even than Jacob. A woman grown, or near enough, but slender like a blade of grass.

Jacob continued, "And where's the nearest train station? Days away. We won't turn back, and we can't wait here."

Hopeful agreed, "Of course you can't. What's to stop us from adding you to our train?" She raised her eyebrows.

"Wallace won't like it," Ness said.

"And who hired him for his pathfinding know-how?" She tilted her head to one side.

"Your pa agreed that Wallace does the deciding. You know that."

"I know that."

"Wallace gets the last say. He always does. Make no mistake on that."

Hopeful smiled. "I am not suggesting we should mutiny, Ness. I mean we ought to bring him into this discussion, is all."

Ness glanced over at the circled wagons. "Seems

he agrees."

A man broke through the wagon circle and strode toward us. Tall, slim, and, black-skinned like Ness, Hopeful, and the Reverend Eli. "Glory be," I said under my breath. Was the whole wagon train made up of colored folks?

When Wallace reached us, the Reverend Eli joined our group. He stood behind his daughter, hands on her shoulders.

Wallace had a stern mouth with a black mustache that drooped down on both sides. His eyes measured and studied my and Jacob's faces like signs along the trail he could read.

"I'm Wallace," he said. "I understand you've had trouble. Ness here told me some of it."

Hopeful spoke before Jacob or I could. "I've asked if they want to join us. They need someone to look after them, seven orphaned children alone in the middle of this nowhere land. Don't you think?"

Wallace's lips tightened, and he let out a huff of air from his nose the way a horse snorts at feed it doesn't like. "Are you leading this outfit now, Miss Hopeful?"

She didn't react. I shifted sideways, trying to edge farther from his angry gaze. But not Hopeful. She stood there unmoving, her father's hands on her shoulders like a blessing. "Of course not. We agreed to do as we're told, not do the telling. That's why I asked what you think."

A laugh rose inside me. I could see that she was clever. I shuffled around, covering my temptation to laugh. A laugh would not help our chances of joining this wagon train and finding the only kin we had left. And I knew then that I wanted nothing else.

"What about you, Reverend Eli?" Wallace asked. "Do you think we ought to take on these white children?"

"White or black, we can't desert them in their hour of need." The Reverend Eli's melodious voice spread warm and gentle over us. "'Let the little children come to me, and forbid them not,' that's what the Lord Jesus said. We are to welcome them all, protect and care for them all. Not only our own children. Not only the children of our friends. Not only children who look the same as us."

A seventh person joined us then: the woman I'd seen driving the lead wagon. She didn't walk so much as glide, her dark gray skirt skimming the stubby grass as if she skated over smooth ice. Her skin was lighter than the others', and yet still not the same as our pale skin. Her dark eyes were fringed with eyelashes as long and soft as a foal's. Those eyes slanted upward at the outside corner, matching the way her elegant lips curved up. She was the most beautiful woman I had ever seen. Even now, I can't say that I've seen any to match her. I stared at her openly, unashamedly, and I felt sure nothing could persuade me to focus my eyes elsewhere ever again.

This woman came up beside the Reverend Eli and took his arm, which removed one of his hands from his daughter's shoulders. She smiled around at all of us, and my troubles seemed lifted right off my shoulders. Her beauty and grace proclaimed this woman to be as close to perfect as any sinner could get. Surely, she would agree we should join them, and all would be well. For who could argue with a woman so lovely, so perfect?

"I couldn't help but overhear." Her words were soft and drawn-out, elegant and sweet to my ears.

Wallace touched the brim of his hat courteously. "Mrs. Mallone. Do you want to give your opinion too? Seeing as how everyone thinks this is a democracy today?"

She ignored the edge of sarcasm in his words. "Thank you, Wallace. My husband is right, of course, that we must care for all God's children." Her smile dazzled me, and I noticed that she looked to be far younger than her husband. No wrinkles lined her face. Her hair beneath her lace-edged bonnet was a glossy black. She certainly didn't look enough older than Hopeful to be her mother.

Mrs. Mallone continued, "But I wonder if adding these little ones to our own crowded band would be the best way of serving them? When we meet other whites, might they not question if these seven had come with us of their own free will? If our wagons were detained on suspicion of kidnapping, we could lose precious traveling time. We could meet serious consequences for what we did out of kindness."

Jacob said, "I am old enough that I'll be believed if I say we're traveling with you by choice. I'm nearly seventeen, ma'am. I'm not a child."

I glared at my cousin. He sounded more insulted than he needed to. Couldn't he see that this lovely woman had only our best interests at heart?

Mrs. Mallone said, "I see that now. But I wonder if you and your brothers and sisters might not feel out of place in the midst of so many colored folks?"

Jacob stood straighter. "My sister and brothers and cousins would be honored to join your wagon train. We're already a week behind where we should be. All we ask is to drive along with you until we reach Independence. We can pay you some, too. I think we can find other white folks in Independence that will take us to Kansas, if need be."

Hopeful said, "That's only a few days. I'll watch the littler ones and make sure they don't slow us down more than any of our own young'uns."

Mrs. Mallone smiled. "That is very good of you, Hopeful. But what time can you spare? I'm running low on some of my remedies. I need you to help search out what we can find here in Missouri. I don't know what sorts of plants grow on the other side of that big river. They may be entirely different over there, and I've not studied them. We've only a few days to replace the things I've used already."

I felt a surge of respect for Mrs. Mallone. She not only had the beauty of an angel, but she helped doctor sick folks too? Before I realized what I was doing, I blurted out, "That's a good idea. You never know when folks might take sick. If you'd come along sooner, my aunt and uncle..." My words and voice faded when I realized everyone was looking at me. My cheeks and ears grew hot, and I dropped my eyes. I hated a crowd of people looking at me. Still do. The more people staring, the worse I hate it, like I'm a bug being studied by a curious child.

Hopeful reached over and took my hand. She gave it a gentle squeeze that comforted me somehow. "That's so," she agreed. "These children are smart, I can tell. I can teach them what plants to search for, and they can be of help."

I nodded. "I'd like that." Hopeful squeezed my hand again.

Mrs. Mallone eyed me. "Could you do that? Help my girl find the herbs and such I need? A boy, likely careless and rowdy?"

"I could!" I insisted. "I'm not careless, ask Jacob."

Wallace said, "Never mind that. Who'll drive their

wagons?"

Jacob squared his shoulders. "I've been driving right along. Levi can handle a team too. We'll get by."

I made myself meet Wallace's eyes. I needed him to believe me. "I can do it, sir."

"All day? Every day? Gets mighty wearisome. A boy wants to be running and exploring, not eating the dust of thirty wagons mile after mile."

"I can do it, long as we get to Kansas."

Ness said, "I expect we got enough folks to spell him when his legs need stretching."

Wallace grunted.

Jacob insisted, "We'll take care of ourselves, Mr. Wallace. We won't be a burden, and we won't get in anyone's way. Like I said, we can pay what's right. We've got to reach Kansas and our uncle. I promised my pa and ma we would. If you make us stop at some town or other, people there might try to keep us there, maybe split us up and give us homes, a few here and a few there. I'll not let my brothers and sister be split, nor my cousins. We belong together."

Wallace took a deep breath, huffed it out again, and nodded. "I guess enough of us here have felt the pain of separated families to understand that. All right, we'll try it. Be ready to move in the morning. You can follow the last wagon."

Jacob said, "How much will you take for adding us to the wagon train?"

"Nothing. I'm all paid up for this trip." Wallace tipped his hat to Mrs. Mallone with an apologetic shrug. She gave him a warm smile, as if rewarding him, though I could not fathom for what.

Wallace told Ness, "Let's go, son. We've got plenty to tend to."

Ness tipped his own hat to the ladies and followed Wallace.

Hopeful asked, "You need any help packing up?"

Before any of us could answer, Mrs. Mallone said, "That's kind of you to offer, child, but maybe they don't want a darky handling their things." She looked at Hopeful, eyes narrowed. "Besides, I need your help getting your papa settled for the night." Her voice sweetened as she told her husband, "I worrry that walking all the way over here, and then standing about in the sun for so long might be too much for you. You're trembling like a kitten."

"I hadn't noticed." The Reverend Eli sighed. "I'm sure you're right, Lu. I had no idea I'd stood out here so long."

"Do you think you can make it back to our wagon?" she asked, solicitous and worried. "I don't know what Hopeful and that Ness were thinking, making you stand all this time. I wish I'd realized sooner that they hadn't brought you back."

"I believe I can make it all right, Lu." He patted her hand. "Especially with you to help me."

"Yes, yes, I'll always be near you, Eli, don't you fret." She led him away, gliding at his side all the way to the circled wagons.

Hopeful hung back. "You sure you don't need any help?" she asked again. "When Wallace says be ready to go right off tomorrow, he means it. If you're not hitched up and moving, he'll leave you here. He takes his job serious."

"We can manage." Jacob spun on his heel and stalked away, back straight as a rifle barrel.

"Thank you anyhow, Miss Mallone." I smiled, remembering the way she had squeezed my hand companionably, the way she'd done her best to convince Wallace to take us along.

"Call me Hopeful, won't you please? Miss Mallone sounds too much like Mrs. Mallone, and that's my stepmother's name."

Stepmother. That explained Hopeful's closeness in age to her father's beautiful wife. "Thank you anyhow, Hopeful," I amended.

"You're welcome. Peace be with you, Levi." She walked slowly away over the trampled grass.

CHAPTER FIVE

There's no sense in telling this story if I'm not going to tell it straight. I won't flinch from the truth, much as it embarrasses me now. In truth, I could not get Mrs. Mallone out of my mind. Everything about her had fired my imagination in a way I'd not known before. I thought her the first truly beautiful woman I'd ever seen. I forgot about the pretty girls I'd known back home in Illinois. I failed to recall even the clear, sweet beauty I'd seen in her stepdaughter's face. They all faded, eclipsed by Mrs. Mallone.

I know now that many a boy stretching up toward manhood has felt that pull toward some lovely woman who's crossed his path. Felt something he could not name, a boyish reverence crossed with the male's natural yearning for the female. Time and again, I've seen boys do this. Girls too, idolizing some man who's handsome and strong that they think represents everything a grown man should be.

But at that time, only fourteen and still so unknowing, I supposed those hushed and awestruck emotions were unique to me alone. All that first evening, I cherished the memory of her smile, her voice. If we could travel with them, maybe I could find ways to cross her path again. I scarcely touched my supper, had to be reminded to do simple tasks, and went to bed feeling disconnected from this earth.

Daydreaming about Mrs. Mallone also kept me from thinking about losing Uncle Drew and Aunt Phoebe and baby Andrew. I can see that now. At the time, though, I didn't think it odd that I didn't cry myself to sleep the way I could hear my cousins and sisters doing.

No one sobbed or fussed in a loud way, but I could hear their quiet crying and sniffling above me. Laura and Lillie slept with Martha and the little boys in the wagon with our household goods inside. I slept beneath them, and Jacob rolled himself up in dignified solitude under the other wagon, where Uncle Drew had slept until he took sick. I think I drifted off before any of the others that night.

Next morning, Jacob and I scrambled out of our blankets at first light. He had spared me enough words to make it clear he wanted us part of that train. I made it equally plain I agreed, though I kept my reasons to myself.

None of us spoke much. Martha said no words at all, and the rest of us had enough to do trying to remember all the things Aunt Phoebe and Uncle Drew had done when breaking camp along the trail. Jacob hitched the horses to one wagon while I ate, then I hitched up the other team so he had a chance to eat. The girls burned the bacon, and the corn dodgers never got cooked clear through, but it beat having no breakfast at all.

Over in the circle of wagons, children laughed and hollered. Mothers called back and forth, and boys and menfolk brought their animals past us to water at the stream. I noted that most of them had mules, not horses, to pull their wagons. They gave us a wide berth, and none of them spoke to us, though most looked us over from afar. My mind had not yet gotten over the idea of traveling in company with so many colored folks, and I spent my fair share of time eyeing them too.

I realized Mrs. Mallone had been right. It felt strange having a light face among so many dark ones. As if being an orphan didn't make me feel out of place enough, now we looked different too. It made me uncomfortable.

I'd lived among white people all my life. White people in the small Illinois town where my parents bought our supplies, sold our extra crops, and went to church. White people in the bigger town where Uncle Drew and Aunt Phoebe did the same. And though some might have a ruddy or fair complexion, we mostly all had about the same shade of skin color. Not so with these folks. Some had skin so dark they made me think of shadows wearing clothes. Others had skin the color of wet earth, or milky coffee, or polished leather. I had not expected such variety.

Of course, I'd heard about colored people. My pa and his brother, Uncle Matthew, had both fought in the war to free them. But until then, they'd never seemed real, somehow. Or maybe only half real, like the knights and ladies and outlaws in Aunt Phoebe's book *Ivanhoe* that she read aloud the first winter we lived with them. I'd relished the story of a hero who kept every promise, championed every innocent victim, righted every wrong. Something in me had needed that story, and I clung to it.

By the time Ness rode up on his big bay, Jacob and I sat high atop our respective seats, reins in our hands. Ness drew up alongside Jacob and ordered, "Follow the last wagon."

The circled wagons groaned to life, rolling onto the trail one after another. My sisters waited beside me, but Martha took Henry and Caleb to stand by their parents' graves, staring down at the two dirt mounds. I remembered then how it had felt to leave our churchyard after my mother's burying. Uncle Drew had let me ride his horse with him instead of riding in the wagon with the other children. I expect it was the only way he could lure me into leaving without a fuss. I figured Martha and the little ones would fuss now.

But when Jacob swung in behind the last wagon, Martha took her brothers by their hands and ran to catch up. I started my team behind him, my sisters lagging a bit until Martha and the little boys joined them. We moved at a slow, steady pace even five-year-old Caleb could keep up with for a while. When he got tired, he'd get to play in the wagon I drove. Seven-year-old Henry would have to walk longer. Every pound we could spare the horses was a mercy and a necessity. We depended on them in a desperate way.

You might think it would be better to ride, driving the team. But those walking could spread out, away from the dust clouds stirred up by the wagon train. Back when we'd traveled with our first train, I'd run about with the younger children. Uncle Drew had driven one wagon, and Aunt Phoebe and Jacob had taken turns driving the other.

I'd known it would be dirty work. I'd seen how gritty and dry the folks at the end of our train had gotten. But I hadn't understood how it would feel.

Fine dust in my mouth and nose, sifting through my cotton bandanna. Grit in the corners of my eyes, in my ears, all through my hair. When we stopped for a noon meal, I felt as if my own flesh might change back into the dust that coated me.

No one wants to be last in a wagon train. You eat the dust of everyone in front of you, every hoof of every horse and ox and mule. You literally eat it, even when you wear a bandanna up over your mouth and nose the way Jacob and I did. Last place in the train is for the lowliest of the lowly. Wallace was telling us we were hangers-on, unwanted and barely welcome, and he didn't need one single word to get his message across. Even lost in half-focused daydreams, I still noted this. Noted and accepted it. At least he allowed us to tag along.

When the wagons stopped at noon, I halted my team too, set the brake, and climbed down, my legs and back stiff from jolting on a wagon all morning. Jacob and I fed and watered the horses. I felt sorry for them. Dust coated them as much as us, and they had no bandannas to keep it out of their noses. We dipped rags in water and cleaned out their noses, hoping that would help some.

Laura found me behind the wagon where I was tending Uncle Drew's riding horse. "Levi, I got something to say you don't want to hear."

"Oh?"

"We ate up all the food at breakfast. All we'd fixed, I mean. None of us thought about noon."

I groaned. I doubted we would stop long enough to light fires and cook. Like our old wagon train, we would halt each day just long enough to feed, water, and rest the stock. Everyone cooked up extra in the morning to eat cold at midday.

"You tell the others yet?" I asked.

"Lillie and Martha. We been trying to think what we could eat quick, but even salt pork shouldn't be eaten without frying it."

"You tell Jacob?"

"No-o-o." She drew the word out and let it linger between us.

"You want me to tell Jacob."

"Might be easier."

"Easier for you. Why can't Martha tell him? He's her brother."

"Martha's not talking still."

I nodded. "I see."

"And here I thought I'd never meet someone with less to say than Jacob."

"Laura—"

She held up both hands. "I know. I'd not say that to her. Or him." She poked my midsection with one forefinger. "But I can say anything to you."

I grinned.

"Still, what about food?" Laura asked.

"Maybe we can trade for some? Might we spare something that someone else could use? One of Aunt Phoebe's dresses?"

"Don't seem right."

"Something smaller. A bonnet?"

"We're keeping what we can of hers for Martha."

"What we *can*."

Before Laura could reply, I heard a voice calling my name. "Levi Dalton! Where are you, Levi Dalton? And Jacob Dalton? Laura? Martha? Where could you be hiding?" I peeked out from behind the right rear wheel.

"There you are at last." Hopeful Mallone headed my way, a basket looped over one arm. "How're you making out way back here?"

"We're all right."

"Dusty?"

I shrugged, disappointed her stepmother wasn't with her. "Yeah, dusty."

"Thought as much. You like apples?" She pulled aside the cloth that covered the basket's contents. Inside, I saw winter apples, shrunken and wrinkled.

I could almost taste them, how they'd be sweet and a bit leathery, good for chewing even though they'd not be juicy anymore. "Apples are my favorite, ma'am. But we don't need your charity."

Laura kicked me.

"Sure you do. Everyone needs charity." Hopeful took an apple from the basket and tossed it my way. "Charity's just another word for love. Everyone needs love, Levi."

I caught the apple. No sense letting it hit the dirty ground, even if I didn't intend to eat it.

"And I told you, call me Hopeful. Don't call me ma'am. It makes me feel old. I don't want to feel old until I'm married and a mama. You can call me Miss if you feel you have to, but I like plain Hopeful. I'm not fancy." She tossed Laura an apple too.

Jacob came out from around the other side of his wagon. "Levi's right. We don't need your charity."

Hopeful faced him. "A gift from a friend is not charity." She took another apple from her basket and held it out to him. "We got a full barrel of these yet. My daddy couldn't bear to leave them behind. They're from the trees he and my mama planted before I was born. But if we don't eat them before the weather heats up, they'll spoil. So, we share them with all our friends. Won't you be our friend, Jacob Dalton?"

I waited and worried that Jacob would turn her down. The apple fitted perfectly in my palm, snug and firm. I couldn't help sniffing it. How pleasingly sweet and full of goodness that apple smelled. My stomach grumbled in agreement.

Jacob kept right on frowning. But he reached out and took that apple from her, then retreated around the wagon again. A moment later, his little brothers arrived, Lillie and Martha trailing behind. Shyly, they accepted apples from Hopeful, and I finally bit into mine. I meant to take small bites so it would last longer, but once I started chomping, I finished that apple in a few mouthfuls. I cleaned the core with my teeth, then tossed it off into the grass.

"Levi!" Hopeful scolded. "We're saving our apple seeds. We'll need apple trees where we're going."

"Sorry." I hunted around until I found the core. When I offered it to Hopeful, I asked, "You going to be the next Johnny Appleseed?"

"It so happens, I am." She took my apple core, then offered me her basket. "Share the rest with the little ones and bring me the basket when you've emptied it." Before I could argue, she strolled off jauntily over the grass.

I munched my second apple more slowly, making sure I saved the seeds for her. Laura took the basket from me and shared the apples out among the others. I managed to snag one more before we had to move on.

All too soon, the time came to climb back up on that wooden seat. One by one, the wagons rolled forward, creaking and groaning. I wanted to groan along with them, but at least my belly was quiet, thanks to our new friend and her gifts. And we hadn't had to tell Jacob that the girls had forgotten to cook enough for the noon meal, either, though I suspicioned he knew anyway.

CHAPTER SIX

Someone up ahead hollered out long and loud, signaling for us to stop for the night. The lead wagon turned off the trail, lurching and swaying over the trail's edge and then running more smoothly over the grass. Jacob and I followed the circling wagons, everyone's teams going slower and slower.

The lead wagon stopped right behind mine, like a snake about to bite its tail. I tingled all over when I realized we'd be right beside the Mallone wagon. Last in line suddenly became the best place to be. Dust and grime didn't matter a jot when compared to the chance of seeing Mrs. Mallone.

Buoyant as a soap bubble, I jumped down and set about my nightly task of unhitching the team. I wished that horses could care for themselves so I'd be free to see if Mrs. Mallone had any need of water fetched or wood gathered. Or someone to talk to, if she'd gotten lonesome driving her wagon all day.

While I worked on those pesky leather straps and buckles, I noticed a young girl about Lillie's size traipsing over to the Mallone wagon. She clutched a handful of wildflowers. I kept my eyes on my work, but I heard Mrs. Mallone murmur a thank-you. Off the girl scampered, a pleased smile spread all across her dark face.

Not two minutes later, a boy came bearing an armful of sticks and twigs. He eyed me sideways as he got closer, but didn't speak. He approached Mrs. Mallone, stacked his bundle of firewood where she indicated, then scurried off when she'd thanked him. I sulked. By the time I got this team unhitched, watered, rubbed down, and picketed, other people would've taken care of Mrs. Mallone's every need, and there'd be nothing left for me to do.

I'd about gotten the second horse unhitched when a third visitor strode across the wagon circle. It was Wallace this time. At first, I thought he was headed for us, maybe to ask how we'd fared. He had two rabbits in one hand and a hunting rifle in the other. Maybe he meant to offer us the rabbits as a sort of apology for having been set against us joining. But no, he also went straight to the Mallone wagon. Mrs. Mallone's voice warmed to a glowing murmur while she thanked him. Wallace replied, and they spoke quietly together for several minutes.

When I finally had the team unhitched and the harness neatly stowed, I led the horses to water and then picketed them for the night next to where Jacob had staked the other team and his pa's riding horse.

Someone had built a good fire not far from our wagons, and I saw my sisters and Hopeful near it in earnest discussion of some important matter which I hoped related to making food. I grabbed Hopeful's basket from where I'd stashed it and joined them.

Right when I reached the fireside, Mrs. Mallone sailed across the grass toward the fire. I held the basket out. "Thank you kindly for the apples, Miss Hopeful." I spoke loud and clear, hoping to impress Mrs. Mallone with my gentlemanly manners.

Hopeful accepted the basket with a smile. "Glad you liked them."

"I saved you all the seeds, too." I scooped those out of my pocket and offered them to her.

Mrs. Mallone joined us. "Oh, dear. Hopeful, you haven't been peddling apples, have you?" she said, her tone reproachful. "You know I don't want you doing that."

Hopeful put my seeds in her apron pocket. "Not peddling. Just sharing, is all." Her voice had lost its smile, though I hardly noticed, for Mrs. Mallone's nearness had taken about all my attention.

She stood close enough I could have reached out and touched her wide, sweeping skirt. It was the color of a new fawn, soft and smooth and comforting. Her skin looked darker by comparison, much darker than it had the day before. But her face had the same enchanting allure, especially with no bonnet concealing or shadowing it.

Mrs. Mallone said, "That's why you had so little time to gather the mullein I asked for. There's still some daylight left. Why don't you see if you can find any before it gets dark."

"Yes, ma'am." Hopeful hurried away

Mrs. Mallone clucked her tongue. "I know she means well." She heaved a sigh, then asked brightly, "Are you children fixing supper?"

Laura said, "We're about to start."

"I'm glad to see you can look after yourselves. I'd feared you would burden the rest of us." She headed back to her wagon.

As if drawn by a string, I followed her. When she noticed me, she asked, "Well? What is it?"

"Oh, I—I—I thought I'd ask if you needed anything, ma'am. Water fetched, or horses rubbed down, or rabbits skinned, anything at all."

She smiled down at me, a smile meant only for my own eyes. A fragile, fleeting gift. "What's your name, child?"

"Levi Dalton, ma'am."

"Levi, I could use some fresh water for my wash basin. Have you a bucket?"

"Oh, yes, ma'am. I'll be right back, ma'am." I whirled and ran for our wagon, snatched up one of our buckets, and ran off to the stream like a frisky colt.

Jubilation at having found a way to serve my new idol gave me such a burst of noisy energy that I whooped the way I imagined an Indian would. Loud, happy, and sudden, my boyish war cry startled a team of horses still watering at the stream.

"Whoa, whoa," came a deep, displeased voice. "Settle down, now." Then up before me loomed the biggest, blackest man I had yet seen. "What're you doing here?" His voice rumbled in my ears like too-close thunder.

"Fetching water," I stared up at him. I felt so small. He could sit down on me and squash me.

"I heard the Reverend Eli took in some white children. White orphans."

I couldn't speak.

"Ain't you one of them white orphans?"

"Yes," I squeaked out.

"I said you'd bring trouble, and I see I was right." He glared down at me, the horses shying away from us both, tugging on their reins. "What do you mean, scaring the Reverend Eli's horses like a devil's after you?"

"I'm sorry."

"I'll show you what sorry means." He raised one

mighty hand. I closed my eyes, preparing myself to get knocked clear to Kansas.

Behind me, Ness said, "Leave him be."

"What's that? What'd you say to me?" growled the other man.

I opened one eye and saw Ness edge around me until he stood clear of us both. His right hand rested gently on the outside of the holster he wore at his side.

"Boy meant no harm. He's fetching water, is all. Made more noise than he needed, but that's a boy for you." Ness spoke easily, the way he would quiet a spooked horse. "And he apologized."

The big man licked his lips, eyeing Ness's gun. "No call for a fuss now, Mr. Ness. I don't aim to cause trouble. You and your pa know I don't."

"I hadn't thought so, until now. But you best remember Wallace said they could join our train. What Wallace says goes. If you don't like it, you can find another train."

"Yes, Mr. Ness. I'll remember it. You tell your pa I will." He looked around, searching for some reason for being there. "Got to get these horses back to Miz Mallone."

"Go on, then," Ness told him.

The big man sidled away, leading the Mallone horses.

I glanced up at Ness. "I didn't mean to."

"Those crazy noises made themselves, did they?" He led his big bay to the stream and let her drink.

"No, I didn't mean to scare the horses."

He grinned at me, teeth white and straight as a knife blade. "I know you didn't."

I knelt upstream from his horse and sank our bucket into the river. "I sure am glad you happened by. Thank you."

"You're welcome. But I might not be around next time. You'd best avoid being away from camp alone, and the same goes for the rest of you. There's some in this train that don't like Wallace and the Mallones taking you along with us."

"Why's that?"

"Most of the folks in this train lived in slavery once, that's why. The grown ones, anyhow. To them, white children are something to look after and worry over. Used to be, white children would grow up to be slaveholders. Some habits don't die easy."

"Weren't you a slave?" At fourteen, the question seemed simple, something to ponder and ask, not words with the potential to wound. At fourteen, the world was a much easier place to walk in.

"No, not that I recall. Not Wallace, either. He was born free out west. And he freed me, you might say."

"Isn't Wallace your pa?"

"He's all the pa I've ever known. He found me when I was too little to remember. Found my first folks dead, along with the white people in the big house. Me, left to die by whoever had killed them all. Thieves, Wallace thought. I've been free since that day."

Even my boyish ears caught the wistfulness in those words. "My folks are dead too," I said. "My *first* folks. But I can remember them. I'm sorry you can't."

Ness's horse finished drinking, raised its head, and snorted water all over Ness's shirt front. "Hey, now!" he laughed. He coaxed the mare away from the stream and headed back to camp. I trudged beside him, lugging my full bucket. "Don't be sorry, Levi. I'll see my folks again, same as you'll see yours. And the Lord gave me all the family I ever needed in Wallace."

"That's how I felt about Uncle Drew and Aunt Phoebe."

"I hadn't thought of that. You've been orphaned twice, haven't you."

"I guess so. But we've still got our Uncle Matthew waiting for us. He's my pa and Uncle Drew's younger brother. He don't know yet about Uncle Drew and Aunt Phoebe, though."

"Like I told your cousin before, you could send him a telegram."

Telegrams were for adults, to my way of thinking. "Jacob could, maybe." Weren't telegrams expensive, though? And we should save the money in Uncle Drew's cashbox for emergencies. The cashbox that

51

was hidden under the seat where Jacob sat driving the team. But then again, them dying might qualify as an emergency.

"I'll speak with Jacob about it, if you want."

"Thank you. I'd never have thought of it. Don't know if Jacob has either." I hesitated, then added, "He don't talk to me much, as a rule."

"And one of the girls don't talk at all, I hear."

"Martha. But that's just since their folks died. Jacob hasn't ever had much use for me, not since we moved in with them."

Ness shrugged. "Some folks don't get along with certain others. Not always a rhyme or reason why. Leading wagon trains, me and Wallace see it all the time. Sometimes you got to work at keeping them apart so they don't tear into each other. Sometimes they do like Jacob, ignore someone." He slowed so I could keep up with him. "Don't forget that it's his parents we left by the trail this morning. Him and the others are doing awful fine considering that."

"I suppose so."

We didn't say much else until we reached the wagons. I had new things to think over, and I've never been one who could think and talk at the same time, not then and not now.

Ness saw me safely back to my sisters, then picked up the two rabbits his father had brought the Mallones. "These won't clean themselves, will they?"

He left with them in one hand, leading his horse with the other.

I hurried on my own way. I set the bucket down beside the wooden steps and climbed up, figuring Mrs. Mallone was inside their wagon, since I didn't see her anywhere. "Mrs. Mallone?" I called out. "Here's your water, Mrs. Mallone."

She had her back to me, seated at the end of the wagon. She was putting something into a polished wooden box. When I called her name, she closed the box's lid before looking out of the opening in her wagon's canvas covering. "Thank you, child. Leave it right there by the wheel, and you can take your bucket when I'm through."

"There anything else you need?"

"Not now." She laid a finger on her lips. "I've just given my husband his sleeping draught. We must be quiet so he can get some rest."

"Oh!" I whispered. "I see." It was awful early for a grown man to go to sleep, for the sun had not yet set. But I'd sensed that the Reverend Eli was not a well man and, of course, sick people always need more rest. "That's handy you can doctor him up."

"It is, isn't it?"

I backed away and nearly collided with my sister Lillie.

"What's the matter with you?" she asked, her voice high and loud.

"Nothing," I said. "You hush now. The preacher needs rest." I led her back to the cooking fire.

Laura greeted me with a scowl. "Where have you been? I needed you to fetch water so I can boil up these potatoes and things."

"I just fetched some." I turned back around in time to see Mrs. Mallone pour some of my water in a deep basin set on top of the steps leading up to her wagon. She tossed the rest on the grass.

I sighed. "And I'll be fetching some more now, won't I." I remembered Ness's warning not to go far alone. "Guess I'll go find Jacob and we'll bring you back enough water for the cooking and washing up both." I told her what Ness had said about us not going places alone, though I left out my encounter with the angry man. Then I reclaimed my empty water bucket. Mrs. Mallone busily patted her face dry with a flour sack dyed bright yellow. When she saw me, she nodded twice, more to herself than as a greeting or thanks for me.

CHAPTER SEVEN

None of us Daltons slept much that first night with the new wagon train. Jacob wanted to change our sleeping arrangements, that was the trouble. Or, that started it, anyway. Always before, Uncle Drew had slept under one wagon, and Jacob and I had slept under the other. Aunt Phoebe, the three girls, and the little boys had all crowded into the wagon full of our personal effects.

Aunt Phoebe had planned it all out when we first loaded up the wagons back at their farm. She put a thin mattress ticking for Martha and my sisters at one end of the wagon and another for herself and her three youngest at the other, both on top of all the boxes, crates, and trunks that held our family goods. Remembering all the care she took to arrange the wagon just right made me miss her so much, I felt like I'd swallowed one of the little boys' wooden blocks and it was stuck in my chest.

When we hauled out our blue woolen blankets, Jacob told me, "You'd best sleep under the farming wagon." All around us, colored folks were getting ready for sleep too. Women sang soothing songs I'd never heard before.

"Why?" I disliked the idea of sleeping alone, away from my sisters and cousins and surrounded by strangers. "Last night I slept here same as always." We kept our voices low so as not to disturb anyone. We had all agreed, almost without words, that we'd do everything we could not to be a bother to anyone. I'd told Jacob about the angry man.

"We'll take turns, then." Jacob's voice was harsh, his words so short he must have bitten off parts of them and kept them inside. He tossed his blanket under the wagon he'd chosen, claiming it.

From inside that wagon came the sounds of Laura and Lillie helping Martha get the two little boys changed and settled. My sisters spoke softly, and they hushed the boys' shrill voices over and over. Caleb kept asking them, "Where's Mama?" until I'd have thrown him out if I'd been my sisters.

Still, I didn't want to be away from them. "We can both sleep under this one like we used to."

"Got to guard both wagons. You know that."

"You really think I can guard a wagon?" On any ordinary day, that knowledge would have pleased me. It meant Jacob didn't hold me entirely worthless after all. But not right then. I wanted nothing more than to stay close to other people when the cooking fires burned out and the land had nothing left to light it but a young moon and the stars.

"Anyone tries getting up in there, you can holler out, can't you?" Jacob rummaged around in the farm goods wagon, then brought out Uncle Drew's rifle. For a moment, I thought he would give it to me. But instead, he laid it on his own blanket.

A warning holler. That was all Jacob thought me good for. Even a child could do that. I clenched my blanket, twisting it back and forth in my hands. "You sleep under there, then, if you think someone might steal our old plow or the cookstove."

"Ain't the plow and cookstove I'm worried about. Besides, I got to stay close in case Martha needs help with Henry and Caleb and An… anything."

He'd almost said *Andrew*. It wrenched something loose inside me, not ever again being able to say Andrew's name after Caleb's.

"Martha has both my sisters helping her." My voice rose higher and louder. "What help would you be with Henry and Caleb? You pay them no mind most times. Why start noticing them now? You think you're the boss of us now, so go ahead and sleep where Uncle Drew slept." I was almost yelling by then. "You guard our plow and stove and… things!"

I'd almost said "money," but I remembered in time that we'd all vowed never to speak of that around anyone not named Dalton.

Part of the money belonged to me and Laura and Lillie, all that was left from selling our farm after our folks died. Our aunt and uncle had dipped into it to buy us shoes and such a few times, but most of it lay safe in that box, along with what Uncle Drew got for selling his farm and stock a month earlier. That money was our new life, all tied up neat and tidy, wrapped in a bit of calico and safe in a metal cashbox hidden under the seat.

"Fine, I will." Jacob pulled out the rifle and his blanket and stalked past me. He pushed them under the other wagon, sliding in after them.

I flung myself down on my back beneath the wagon. Henry and Caleb wailed together, insistent with their need for comfort. The boards above me barely muffled their cries. Laura and Lillie spoke soothingly, and Laura tried crooning a lullaby, but the boys drowned out her singing.

Then a thin, throbbing noise joined them. Not a crying, and not even a wailing, but the sound of a heart breaking, comfortless and lonesome. I knew it must be Martha, giving her wordless grief a voice at last.

Somehow, her keening brought my own tears to the surface. They slid down my cheeks. Puddled in my ears. Slithered on down my neck and made me shudder. Wet the grass beneath me. I rolled onto my side and curled up around the blanket I still clutched, hugging it like a friend.

Above me, five voices wept and sobbed and wailed now, for my sisters had grief of their own to voice. I kept my own crying soft and silent, not wanting anyone to know. Not wanting Jacob to know, in particular.

I should have let Jacob sleep there the way he'd wanted. Ness had said it must seem as though my sisters and I had been orphaned all over again, but this grief was different from what I'd felt when my parents died. Less savage, even if everything looked more hopeless now. My cousins had a deeper grief than my sisters and I did. Jacob should have slept near his brothers and sister. That's why he'd wanted to swap. Just to be near them. I realized it too late.

Soft footsteps padded through the grass nearby. I hiccupped and swiped my eyes with both hands. Had someone come to rob the wagon the way Jacob feared?

As the footsteps neared, I could see they belonged to a woman in a long skirt. She walked straight to the wagon I lay under, knocked twice on its side, then called, "May I come up?" I'd only heard that voice for the first time the day before, but I knew that it belonged to Hopeful Mallone.

One of the girls made it clear through the crying that yes, she was welcome. The wagon tipped and creaked above me as Hopeful climbed in. I could hear her soothing them, though I could not hear her words. While all of them quieted down from wails to muffled sobbing, she began singing. I didn't know the song, but I picked out words about chariots and home and a band of angels. She sang it over and over, soft and gentle.

I fell asleep to the sound of her low, sweet voice without even noticing my tears had stopped.

CHAPTER EIGHT

I woke late in the morning. No trumpet call woke me before sunrise like in our old wagon train. No men tending stock, no women getting breakfast, no children scurrying about their chores. A few people moved around, stirring embers of last night's fires to build them up so they could cook. But the sun had almost finished sliding out of bed herself. We should have all been long awake and busy. Was the whole train afflicted with fever?

I shivered, gazing about in bewilderment. Jacob was gone from under the other wagon. Why had he let me sleep? Did he have the fever too now? Would I never stop losing my family, until I'd left six more graves behind me? Was there no medicine to save them, no doctoring we could do?

I spun in a slow circle, panic clawing its way up my throat. Wagon trains shouldn't be all quiet and sleepy in the morning. Not unless a storm blew up too fierce to move through. But the day dawned fair.

Something must be wrong. I looked desperately for Ness, Hopeful, Mrs. Mallone, the Reverend Eli—anyone whose name I knew! I would even have asked Wallace if he'd been handy, though he scared me with his grim decisiveness.

But I knew none of the women tending the fires, none of the children scattered about. The memory of my encounter at the river with that angry man kept me from seeking out a stranger for answers.

Where was Jacob? He'd not left us, had he?

Behind me, the wagon creaked. I whirled around and saw Hopeful slip quietly out, her hair a little frizzy and her dress wrinkled. She must have stayed all night with my grieving sisters and cousins.

"Hopeful?" I cried. "What's wrong?"

"Wrong where?" She yawned and stretched her arms over her head.

"Everywhere! Nobody's awake, nobody's up and doing things—is there fever?" I felt cold at the thought of digging more graves. Lillie had hardly gotten her feet back under her. What if she caught a fever again, and... no, I couldn't even think that.

Hopeful smiled. "It's just Sunday, Levi."

"Sunday?"

"You know, Sunday. Lord's Day. The day of rest."

"Rest?"

62

"Rest. For us, for the livestock—for everyone but my daddy. He'll be preaching after breakfast. I'd best stir up the fire."

"You mean, we won't move on this morning?"

"Not until tomorrow." She grinned. "Every week, Wallace grumbles about it, but I got the feeling he enjoys the day same as the rest of us. After the preaching, him and Ness and a few others will go out and hunt."

"Oh." I leaned against the wagon, emptied out with relief that there was nothing at all wrong. No fever. No graves to dig.

Jacob came out from behind the wagons. "You're awake. Horses need watering, and the girls will want fresh water too." He handed me one of the two buckets he carried. Then he saw Hopeful kneeling beside the fire, poking at the coals with a stick. He gave me the other bucket and crossed over to her.

Jacob dropped to his heels beside Hopeful. "I want to thank you for caring for my family."

"Somebody's got to," she said, her tone sharp.

"I know. I just... I can't seem to..."

"You'll find yourself, Jacob. Until you do, I'll help keep them alive and well. But we'll be parting ways sooner or later. Don't take overlong."

Find himself? What had she meant by that? How could you lose your own self? I wondered about that all the way to the nearby river.

When we returned with the water, Mrs. Mallone met me at the foot of her wagon's stairs. "Why, thank you, Levi. You fetched my water without me even having to ask."

I straightened up, standing tall with my chest out and my head up like a soldier. "You're welcome, ma'am!" I replied in my most grown-up manner.

"I can see you'll be a handy boy to have around," she told me. "Very handy indeed."

"Thank you. If you've got anything else needs fetching, or maybe help gathering those plants you told Hopeful to get, I'd be proud to help."

She smiled, her lips turning up slowly like she had a secret. "That is most gentlemanlike of you. I will take you up on that." She took the bucket from me. "Maybe later on today. In fact, I can think of several uses for you, never fear."

I nearly floated back to where my sisters huddled around our campfire, stirring something thick in our big cooking pot. Corn meal mush as usual, I knew. Right then, the praise from Mrs. Mallone sweetened everything in my world, even the thought of eating mush yet again.

After eating their breakfasts and caring for the livestock, people drifted toward the Mallone wagon carrying an assortment of blankets, chairs, and stools. Laura washed our breakfast things in our big tub, Lillie rinsed them in a bucket of clean water, I dried, and Martha stacked them in their crate. The people passed us without speaking. Some stared openly, and others looked past us as if we were a mirage. But not one spoke to us.

I didn't try to hide my own watching of them as they set up their meeting place under the clear sky there inside the circle of wagons. Families with children spread blankets in front and settled down on them, their little children clustered close. Older folks with chairs and stools arranged themselves behind. All talked in soft, cheerful voices. Everyone had the appearance of expecting something pleasant and important. They congregated as far from us as they could, all facing the Mallone wagon. We finished our washing up and retreated to the shade of our own wagons, leaving a gap between us and them.

Hopeful stepped down out of their wagon first. "What a fine morning!" she called, raising her arms. "Let's praise the Lord for this morning!" As one, the people seated before her rose.

Scattered cries of "Praise the Lord!" came back from the crowd. Together, they engaged in a sort of call-and-response chanting, rhythmic and somehow musical even without a melody.

Meanwhile, Mrs. Mallone came out of their wagon, holding her husband's hand as he descended the stairs carefully. Though wearing the same dark gray dress I'd seen that first day, she had added a cameo brooch and black lace shawl to fancy it up some. She'd twisted her hair up and piled it into a crown.

When they stood on firm ground, the Reverend Eli straightened his shoulders and walked out to stand beside his daughter. He held his wife's arm for support, and she patted his hand, the perfect image of a loving helpmeet. Hopeful slipped away to the shadow of their wagon.

"How has the Lord been good to you?" the Reverend Eli called to the people.

Everyone responded in their own way, words and voices tumbling over each other with their joy. Some raised their arms and swayed.

I stared. This kind of worship seemed so different from any churchgoing I'd ever done. Back home, we sat in rows, we sang songs out of a hymn book, we recited the familiar liturgy week in and week out, and we listened. I'd always taken that comforting, orderly sameness for granted. I'd had no notion that others might worship another way.

Hopeful saw us and motioned for us to join her, but we made no move to go nearer or participate. I knew many of those folks did not welcome our presence. How might they react if we tried joining their church service? Besides, I saw the large, angry man from the river on the far side of the crowd, standing with his powerful arms crossed over his chest. I'd learned he was a blacksmith named Samson. Being a blacksmith made him important to everyone, for he kept the animals shod and the wagons repaired. Most folks respected him, and I'd seen him smile at little colored boys and girls during supper the night before. But I wanted to stay out of his way all the same. Just because he was respected by others, even liked, that didn't mean he wasn't dangerous to me.

The Reverend Eli prayed, his voice lilting up and down with a gentle cadence as he thanked the Lord for delivering his people time and again. While he spoke, the people chorused their amens, some soft and some loud, not waiting for his prayer to end before they joined in.

Holding out one hand toward his daughter, the Reverend Eli stepped away from his wife. Hopeful walked forward and took her place between them. Mrs. Mallone moved away until she stood in the shadow Hopeful had left.

And then Hopeful sang, sweet and strong: "Jehovah, hallelujah! The Lord will provide." After that first line, everyone else joined in, singing about how foxes had holes and birds had nests, but the Son of God had nowhere to lay his weary head. I recognized those words, remembering them from

67

sermons gone by, but they'd never meant so much to me before.

We had no home now, not even a hole or a nest, and neither did any of these people. We had only our wagons rolling over Missouri, aiming for homes we had not built yet, land we had not seen yet, not knowing where we'd stop each night. And the Lord knew how that felt.

That was a comfort, I found. A comfort I hadn't realized I needed. A comfort I've carried with me ever since, everywhere I've gone.

The people clapped in time with the song, and Henry and Caleb joined in. Hopeful looked over our way and smiled at us as she sang and clapped. The song went on and on, the same few lines over and over, now rising higher in joy, now falling quieter in reverence. My sisters swayed back and forth to the music, and Laura softly sang along.

When the song died down, Hopeful called out, "We're all God's children here, aren't we?"

"We're all God's children here!" the people called back.

"God loves all his children!" she cried.

That got a wider variety of responses: "Amen!" "Hallelujah!" "Thank the Lord!"

"Then let us welcome all God's children as He welcomes them!" Stepping lightly around the crowd, Hopeful came over and took Henry and Caleb by their hands. She led them to the gathering, and the girls and I followed until we all stood beside the front row of blankets.

"Reverend Eli," Hopeful called, "what did the Lord Jesus say about bringing children to Him?"

The Reverend Eli's face lit up with love and kindness. "Forbid them not! For we know of such is the kingdom of heaven." He smiled at my cousins, my sisters, and myself. "Welcome, children, in the name of the Lord Jesus. Peace be with you." He faced his congregation. "Peace be with you, I say!"

"Peace, peace," they called back. Many eyed us warily, but none made any moves to shoo us away.

"Let us pray," he said.

Obediently, my cousins and siblings and I bowed heads and folded hands and closed eyes.

"Lord Jesus, bless all your children, large and small. Fill our hearts with your love and our minds with your truth. Thank you, Jesus, for bringing us to the aid of these little ones. Bless them through us, and bless us through them. Bring us all safely to our journey's end. Let all God's people say amen!"

"Amen," the people chorused, though with less enthusiasm than previously. I noticed none of them had spoken out during this prayer the way they had during the other.

At some unseen signal, they all sat down again, so we sat on the grass too, off to one side. Hopeful settled beside Laura, who held Henry on her lap. Without my noticing, Ness had joined us, and he sat down cross-legged on the other side of Hopeful. He caught my eye and grinned, more cheerful and relaxed than I'd yet seen him.

Then the Reverend Eli preached his sermon. I wish I could recall his words and set them down for you, exactly the way he said them. But they would lack the flavor he put in them, the way his voice started out quiet and gentle, then gradually rose stronger and louder, minute after minute, until he fairly shouted his words, crying them out over all the land as though he wanted to reach even the birds in the sky. Then, like a storm passing away, his words calmed again, until each word seemed a ray of peaceful sunshine inside me.

What did he speak about? God's love, our need for rescuing from our own sin, the many times and ways God had rescued his people on earth, Jesus coming to save us—those are what I can remember, but it felt as though he spoke to each of us about our own private struggles, offering comfort and understanding and forgiveness. When he finished preaching, I felt scrubbed clean inside and out, dressed in new clothes.

More singing and more praying followed, but I remember nothing of that now. During a long prayer after the sermon, my attention wandered until it snagged on Mrs. Mallone. While her husband did his preaching, she had settled on their wagon's wooden steps. I expected her to watch her husband with the same rapt interest as everyone else. Or have her eyes closed and her head bowed the way mine should have been. But she did neither. And her expression reflected none of the peace and joy I felt.

If she hadn't been so beautiful, I would have called her expression ugly, her lips twisted with displeasure. No, more than displeasure—animosity. Why would she glare at her husband that way, when he preached and prayed like an angel stepped down from heaven?

I glanced over at Hopeful. She had closed her eyes and lifted her face to the morning sun, oblivious to her stepmother's sour looks.

I went back to watching Mrs. Mallone and saw her features shift. They went from hateful to shining with beauty quicker than I could have snapped my fingers. Her lips lifted in a smile and her whole face glowed. But she wasn't looking at her husband anymore. I followed her gaze to where Wallace stood at the far end of the crowd. He made no sign he'd seen Mrs. Mallone at all, let alone noticed how her expression had changed.

It all passed beyond my comprehension, and I knew it, so I forced my thoughts back to following the Reverend Eli's prayers.

CHAPTER NINE

After the service, people scattered about camp. Children ran and played in the open center of our circle. We orphans slowly walked back to our own wagons. Where had Jacob been all this time? Off trying to find himself, as Hopeful had mentioned?

Before I could head off to look for Jacob, a little colored boy ran up. He was about the same size as Caleb, barefoot, his britches too short and his shirt sleeves too long. He smacked Henry on the arm, yelled, "TAG!" and darted away again. Henry dashed after him, and Caleb followed, their own bare feet churning up puffs of dust as they joined the flock of other children.

I watched as Henry tagged a girl about his own size, then swooped away, laughing with glee. How good that sounded. I was glad that they could play again, not fear everyone and everything. I wished I could do the same, but I'd outgrown the game long ago. Or maybe it had only been a month or two. Sometimes it felt like years since we'd left the farm. Since I'd really felt like I was still a youngster.

Maybe I could find Mrs. Mallone. Ask her what had bothered her so much during the service. Ask if there might be a way I could help. I don't know now what made me think I'd be able to help, fourteen and shy. Maybe I'd read about King Richard and all that chivalry once too often. Maybe I thought I was the hero of *Ivanhoe*. I'd read Aunt Phoebe's copy over and over. Now, it lay in the trunk with my clothes, heading to Kansas right along with us. Aunt Phoebe had told me when we packed up that it might as well be mine since I'd read it so often.

I saw Ness standing with Hopeful, his head bent down toward her. They were deep in conversation, close and confidential, and I didn't want to interrupt and ask if they'd seen Mrs. Mallone. So I made for the Mallone wagon, figuring she had taken the Reverend Eli back inside. As I neared it, Wallace approached their flight of steps from outside the circle. Since he frightened me, I ducked behind our wagon's back wheel, hoping he'd not see me.

He didn't. He knocked on the side of their wagon and called out, "Reverend Eli? Miz Mallone? We'll be going hunting soon. Is there anything you folks got a hankering for?"

Mrs. Mallone answered him immediately. "Shh, the Reverend is worn out from preaching. He needs his rest," she said, loud enough for me and anyone else around to hear. She reached out one hand for Wallace to take as she descended the steps, skirts gathered daintily in her other hand. "I thank you for your offer, Mr. Wallace." Then, still holding onto him, she led him to the far side of the wagon, outside the circle. There, she spoke softly, her words too quiet for me to hear. She did not take her hand from his.

Wallace gazed down at her, his expression a good match for how mine must have looked whenever I beheld her: awestruck by her beauty, incredulous that she would pay him some measure of attention, and hungry for more time to bask in her presence.

I was spying. I knew it. I knew I should either make myself seen or leave altogether, but I stayed there behind our wagon's wheel. As I watched, I felt a surge of envy. I'd wanted to do something to make her smile at me, but she kept spending her smiles on him instead.

Finally, she stopped speaking and took a step backward. Wallace raised her hand to his lips, turned it over, and kissed her palm, courtly as any knight of yore. Then he strode away, all brisk and busy again.

Mrs. Mallone sidled off, and I was left alone to ponder what I'd seen. Mrs. Mallone was a married woman. Her husband lay napping in the wagon right there, and yet she'd had a whispered conversation with another man, clearly hiding their exchange from the rest of the settlers. She'd held his hand, even let him kiss hers. Something inside me insisted this could not be right.

But no, I insisted back. Mrs. Mallone was the most obviously perfect being I'd ever beheld. That had been no secret tryst. She'd talked quietly so her husband could rest. I knew nothing at all about colored folks, after all—maybe they had a custom of kissing a woman's hand when you took your leave.

Now that Wallace had gone, Mrs. Mallone might have time to talk with me. I scurried off to find out if she did.

Mrs. Mallone did favor me with a smile that day. In the early afternoon, she called me over and sat down on her wagon's stairs. Beside her, she placed a straw basket filled with what looked like dried weeds. That same wooden box rested on her lap, the one I'd seen in her wagon when I first brought her a bucket of water. This was no rough crate such as we used for packing our tin plates and cups, but a polished box of dark wood with a close-fitting, hinged lid. Its glossy sides promised untold treasures within.

"It's good of you to offer your assistance, Levi." She smiled when she said my name.

I felt goosebumps rise up all along my arms.

"Heaven knows I have tried and tried to get my girl to help me, but she's more interested in flitting about the camp, peddling apples."

I said nothing, but stood beside her, eager to see inside that box. Something about it teased me with an unnamed longing.

"I need you to promise me something, Levi." Mrs. Mallone caressed the box with her fingertips, tracing little circles all along its lid. "You must never open this yourself, nor use what I keep in it without my instructions. These are powerful remedies, some of them. And some wouldn't hurt a kitten, no matter how much a body took. But you won't know the difference until you've studied them for years and years the way I have. You promise?"

"I promise."

"I'll know if you break your word. I keep a strict accounting of everything in here." She raised the lid and let me peer inside.

Dark green fabric lined the box, soft and almost furry. I didn't know the name for it then, but now I know it was velvet. Nestled inside the deep, square pockets stood three rows of glass bottles, squarish instead of round, each about four inches high and maybe three inches across. Twenty-one bottles, all stoppered with a cork and a rag stuffed in their wide mouths.

Mrs. Mallone touched the tops of those bottles tenderly. "Each one has a purpose. Each one is a friend," she said softly, almost chanting the words. Then she pulled out one bottle and held it up so I could see inside it. A coarse brown powder filled it nearly to the top. "Dogwood bark for headaches." She returned the bottle to its nest and took out another one half-filled with dry, crumbling leaves. "Raspberry leaves," she told me. "Steeped in water, they help ease a woman's passage into motherhood."

I gazed at those herbs in their bottles, all of them promises of suffering eased or ended, and an idea came to me. Maybe not an idea. Maybe a need I had no name for yet. "What's this one?" I pointed at a bottle filled with a grainy white powder.

"Cotton root."

"What's it do?"

"Nothing you need ever know about." She took out two bottles, one empty and the other nearly so. "Here's our work, Levi. I finally convinced my girl to gather some fresh mullein." She gestured behind her, where long stalks with many leaves hung upside down from the canvas wagon top. "It's got to dry now, but I have some here we gathered a while back. It's dried at last, and I need it safe in my medicine chest."

"What's it for?" I asked.

"Coughing. You make a tea out of the leaves or flowers, and maybe some honey or molasses if you got any, and it'll soothe the harshest cough. Fresh or dry, it works both ways. Now, a poultice made with the fresh leaves will ease the pain of a bad bruise. There are all kinds of uses for mullein."

She gave me one bottle, then pulled a stiff, leafy stalk from the basket. "You take these smaller leaves, even the tiny ones." She showed me the sizes she meant. "Slide them into the bottle, one at a time, as many as you can. If they crumble some, that's all right. But whole is easier to steep."

"I understand." I took the stalk from her and stripped off the littlest thick, fuzzy leaves. I held the unstoppered bottle between my knees where I could poke them down inside it. "Where'd you learn this much about remedies?" I asked.

"From my grandmother. She had a garden filled with plants. Folks would come from all around New Orleans to buy her tonics. She saved up that money and bought her freedom, years before, when she was young enough that any children she bore could be born free. And she taught me all she knew." Mrs. Mallone filled the second bottle. She hummed softly, a song I didn't recognize.

After a couple of minutes, she said, "Truth is, I had a garden well on its way to being as good as hers had ever been, but I had to leave it behind. Like we left everything else." Her voice sounded smooth still, but with a bitterness around the edges now.

"Can't you plant another? I hear dirt in Kansas will grow anything."

"That sort of garden takes time. I brought along what seeds I could, but I'll be starting all over. It'll take years. Still, sometimes starting all over again is necessary. Sometimes you got to bid farewell to one life and welcome another."

She smiled down at the bottle I held. "Good. You learn quickly." She had filled her own bottle already and put it back into its slot in her box. Now she fiddled with the other bottles while I worked, lifting them out one after another and examining them to see how much was left.

All too soon, I'd finished. I had another question, but I worried I would not get the answer I wanted. So I handed her the full bottle without words.

"Thank you." Mrs. Mallone tucked the bottle into its slot. "This eases my mind, knowing I'll have what I need to soothe any coughs folks may develop. My husband sometimes suffers from a cough. Surely you've heard him."

"If you had bigger bottles, couldn't you carry more?" I wondered, even though that was not the question I wanted to ask.

"True. But some of these don't keep for long. A

bigger bottle might mean bigger waste."

I touched the box's smooth side with one finger. "And they'd not fit in your box."

"Not so many nor so well."

Reverently, I ran my finger down the wood. The box was several inches taller than those bottles. And my finger found a change in the grain before my eyes perceived that the bottom inch looked subtly different. "What's this?" I asked. "A drawer?"

Mrs. Mallone laughed, but it was not a happy sound. "Clever boy," she said softly. "Yes, yes, it's a drawer. But I'll not show you how to open it. That's where I keep the dangerous medicines. Things only for a time of the direst need. Things that can cure the right person or destroy the wrong one. Bring a body back to health or send it off to its final resting. Best you forget all about that drawer, Levi."

"Yes, ma'am." I dropped my hand, feeling I'd somehow trespassed against an unspoken rule.

"You're mighty interested in my cures," Mrs. Mallone observed.

My new need rose up in me, putting my question out in the world before I could stop it. "Could I learn how to cure people?" I blurted.

Mrs. Mallone took in a deep breath, then let it out as a lingering sigh. "You're thinking of your folks that died."

"Yes. If you... if someone like you had come by

when they first took sick... if only someone had had medicine..." My thoughts chased each other, coming out half-formed. "We had a sawbones back home, but he didn't know how to help my pa, he wasn't a real doctor. I know you're not a real doctor either, but you know... more than me, anyhow. Maybe if I could learn from you, then that'd be a start. Maybe I could help you, and learn from you, and... and that'd be better than not knowing anything at all about sicknesses." I looked away, embarrassed at having said so much, so badly.

"I see. I do see." Mrs. Mallone considered my idea. "I've never had an assistant. I try teaching my girl, but she's got no interest."

I glanced up, hoping.

"In the evenings, before you turn in for the night, come see me. If I'm not too busy or too tired, I'll teach you what I've got time for."

My words deserted me. I nodded, enthusiastic and grateful.

"You got to understand, though, not everything has a cure. Why, even though I'm a healer, my own first husband still took sick and died, and that's the truth."

"I understand."

"Run along, now," she told me, dismissing me with a wave. She rose and took her box back inside, leaving the remains of the mullein in the basket on the steps.

I wandered out to where we'd picketed our stock. Uncle Drew's riding horse was gone, and I figured that meant Jacob had taken him for a pleasure ride or maybe gone hunting with Ness and Wallace. What would Jacob say if I told him I meant to learn how to heal sick folks? Maybe even go to school and learn how to be a real doctor, one far-off day when I was a man full-grown. Or become a healer, like Rebecca in *Ivanhoe*. Like Mrs. Mallone.

I worried Jacob might laugh. But he'd probably shrug and forget it. No sense telling him at all.

CHAPTER TEN

I trudged slowly back to camp, kicking at clods of dirt so I could watch them crumble with a puff of dust. The land there was dry, but I could see that water lurked near the surface, for the landscape held plenty of scattered trees, bushes, and grass. It was good for traveling this way, not so muddy like it would have been a month or so earlier.

Near our camp stood a ring of five trees that my sisters had told me would make a perfect spot for a picnic or a fairy revel. With my mind still half caught up in imagining myself a doctor healing people of a fever or a pox, I wandered toward it. If I'd been much younger, I'd have imagined it into my hospital, and the trees my five patients that needed tending. But I believed that fourteen was too old for such nonsense as pretending.

When I got closer, I heard someone crying. At

first, the muffled sound seemed to come from the trees themselves. I finally remembered that I wasn't supposed to wander about alone. I backed away, thinking I'd best not disturb anyone in distress. But I stepped on a stick that snapped loudly.

"Who's there?" asked a voice soggy with tears.

"I'm sorry! I'm leaving," I babbled. "I didn't mean to intrude. I didn't know you were here. I'm leaving."

"That you, Levi?" Hopeful Mallone stepped out of the trees. She wiped her eyes with her sleeve. "Did my stepmother send you?"

"No. I was just... walking."

Hopeful sniffed and wiped her cheeks with both hands. "Me too. Just walking."

"Walking and thinking," I added.

"All I do lately is walk and think."

I didn't know what to say.

Hopeful hugged her arms around herself. "You seen Ness?"

"Not since he talked with you after the service."

She made a sound that might have been a laugh or a scoff.

"Are you all right?" I asked.

"Oh, yes, Levi. I'm fine. I always have a good cry when the day's going just as it ought. Don't you?"

I'd asked the wrong thing. I wanted to leave. But I could see tears still glistening in the corners of her dark eyes and I didn't want to make them fall. She'd been so kind. "Do you want me to go? Or would you like to talk? Would it help to walk and talk instead of walk and think?"

Hopeful pursed her lips and looked me in the eye. "What's the use?"

"Never mind." I turned away.

"Levi, wait." She caught up with me and took my arm gently, the way a girl would hold the arm of her escort. "I'm sorry."

"That's all right." We strolled outside the wagon circle. "Is it us? Me and my sisters and cousins? Are we causing trouble?"

"You? No. No, y'uns are fine."

"I thought people might still be angry. About us joining the train, I mean."

"If they are, they're wrong. And if they are, they haven't said anything to me. No, this is nothing but foolishness, I expect." Slowly, she shook her head. "You think you're getting to where you really know a person. Then they up and ask you something you never wanted them to say. Or maybe you did, but you knew it wouldn't be of any use."

"Oh."

"That's what I get for being a dreamer, Levi. I start imagining how the world could be. How my life could be. Then when something happens, when it all changes..." She shrugged. "All it ruins are hopes and dreams, not reality. I ought not to cry. I ought to be contented with my life how it is. I see the seven of you and I think, at least I've still got my daddy. They've lost so much more than me, and they're still standing."

"You've got your stepmother too, taking good care of your pa and you. That must be a comfort."

"It must, must it? It looks that way, I suppose." Hopeful pursed her lips. "You like my stepmother, don't you."

"Oh, yes," I assured her. "She's said she'll teach me about medicines and remedies." I looked down, shy about admitting my secret new hope. "I'd like to help folks as she does. Sick folks, I mean."

"Levi, don't get attached to her, you hear?"

"What do you mean? She ain't sick, is she?"

"Not the way you'd think." Hopeful sighed. "She's a selfish woman, Levi. She'll take your help. She'll take and take and take. But she won't give much in return. Maybe nothing. Maybe worse than nothing."

I frowned. "You can't mean that. She isn't selfish at all."

"You can't see it, I suppose. There are times I wonder..." She sighed. "But that's exactly what I have to stop. Stop wondering and dreaming. Even hoping." She laughed, short and bitter. "Maybe I'd better change my name."

Ahead of us, three horsemen rode into view from behind a copse of trees. I recognized Jacob on Uncle

Drew's saddle horse and Ness on his big bay mare. I figured the other would be Wallace, but he lagged behind the others, so I couldn't tell. Both Jacob and Ness had deer slung across their saddles. We'd have fresh meat aplenty that night.

Hopeful saw them too. Without another word, she rushed off.

When I'd finished off my third plate of fried venison and potatoes, I leaned back against the wagon wheel with a contented sigh. The smell of fresh meat fried and roasted mixed with the familiar scents of woodsmoke and coffee. All around the camp, people sang, children chattered, and plates and utensils clinked pleasantly. I think now that I would've been almost happy myself if I hadn't started missing Aunt Phoebe and Uncle Drew and baby Andrew especially much right then.

And I worried about Hopeful. She hadn't come out of her tent beside her parents' wagon for supper. Mrs. Mallone had given Laura an onion and some dried sage to add to our meat and potatoes and taken two plates of food when it was ready. Martha and Laura had cooked our supper, with me peeling the potatoes. Aunt Phoebe had insisted we all learn about cooking, boys as well as girls. She always said we boys might take it into our heads to be prospectors or fur trappers or some such thing when we were grown, which might take us far away from her home-cooked meals. We'd all better know how to fix what food God put in our hands so it'd be fit to eat, that was Aunt Phoebe's rule.

But she would've made rich, hearty venison stew, not fried it a little too black with onions and potatoes that didn't quite get done inside. And she'd have made a pan of biscuits to go along, maybe even two. But none of us had mastered making biscuits in the oven back home, much less over a campfire.

I surely did miss her and Uncle Drew.

To take my mind off them, I said, "I can't figure out what's wrong with Hopeful." Maybe my sisters had found out from Mrs. Mallone when she stopped by for her food.

"She and Ness quarreled," Laura answered.

"What would they fight over?"

Lillie giggled. "Was it a lover's spat?" She tried to whisper, but failed. A ten-year-old girl's whisper is about as quiet as a rooster.

"Hush," Laura scolded. "Be nice."

"Hopeful and Ness?" I asked. "You don't mean they're sweet on each other?"

"I think so. They were talking after the prayer meeting, standing close like I see them do now and then, kind of friendly and shy at the same time. And then Mr. Wallace came over and spoke with Ness and left again. And that's when Ness and Hopeful got in an argument, and Ness stomped off one way, and Hopeful stomped off the other, and that's the last I saw of either of them."

"That doesn't mean anything. Could just be friends. Friends have disagreements."

Lillie smirked. "You mean you ain't noticed? They look at each other the way Jacob used to goggle at Polly Barnes all through church up until she got engaged to that Dover boy."

I remembered that clearly enough. Watching Jacob making cow's eyes at pink-cheeked Polly had been a welcome distraction during longer sermons. "No. Not Ness. Not Hopeful. Not foolish like that."

"No, not foolish like that," Laura agreed. "Sweet."

"Girls." I got to my feet. These were not the sorts of answers I'd been hoping for. I'd wanted something concrete, such as maybe Hopeful broke a dish and got scolded. Not boy-and-girl foolishness. I liked Ness and Hopeful. I wanted to keep liking them. I didn't want to feel I should look away every time they got near each other so I wouldn't catch sight of hand-holding or hear a half-whispered endearment.

I knew I was being unreasonable. It was no business of mine if Hopeful and Ness were sweet on each other. It wouldn't affect us, not for long, at any rate. Why, we'd be in Kansas in a couple of days. Uncle Matthew would meet us there. I'd never see any of the people in this wagon train again.

Maybe losing my aunt and uncle had made me cling to anyone who showed us kindness. Maybe it made me hate the idea of things changing again. And a boy and a girl sweet on each other could lead to changes, I knew that right enough. When people got married, they started new lives, and I had already started life over too often to like the thought of that, little as it might touch me personally.

CHAPTER ELEVEN

I slipped between the wagons, thinking I would check on our horses one last time. We'd picketed them within sight of us, and surely I could go that far unaccompanied without running into trouble.

But before I'd gone five or six steps, Mrs. Mallone stepped out of her wagon and called, "Levi, you seen my girl anywhere?"

I turned back, hoping she might have time to give me another lesson about herbs and remedies. "I think she's in her tent."

"Fetch her for me. I need to fix her hair before it gets too dark."

"Of course!" I hustled back to Hopeful's tent. You can't knock on a tent, especially one that's only a big sheet of canvas slung over a couple of forked sticks and a pole. So, I asked, "Hopeful? Are you awake?" in a voice loud enough to reach through the canvas, but not loud enough to waken her if she really had fallen asleep.

"And if I am?" she replied.

"Your stepmother asked me to fetch you so she can fix your hair."

"Tell her I feel poorly."

"But—"

"That so hard, Levi? Just tell her I feel poorly. It won't be a lie."

I glanced at Mrs. Mallone standing on the top step, a lantern in her hand. She asked sharply, "What's wrong? Where is that girl? She's not run off, has she?"

Twitching aside the tent's door flap, Hopeful stepped out. She had only a loose shift on, with a shawl flung around her shoulders. "I told Levi I feel poorly. Can't we do my hair another day?"

"You know Wallace won't stop us until late tomorrow. He'll want to make up for us not traveling on Sunday. Won't be time then. Best do this now."

"But I'm not dressed."

"It's too dark for anyone to see you. No one around but the orphans, and they're about asleep anyway."

"Very well." With a sigh, Hopeful crossed to the steps.

Her stepmother descended and held out the lantern to me. "Always want to be useful, don't you?"

"Yes." I took the lantern.

"Hold it high for me to see by," she told me. Hopeful sat down on a stool, and I held the lantern where it shone full on her head.

Mrs. Mallone placed a brush and a small crock with a lid on the steps within easy reach of where she stood behind Hopeful. She unwound the strip of cloth that held Hopeful's bun in place, then used her fingers to ease the hair out of its tidy knot. By the light of the lantern, standing that close, I could see that each strand looked like the tiny spring inside Uncle Drew's watch. Jacob's watch now.

As Mrs. Mallone combed through the hair with her fingers, those tiny springs eased apart more and more until Hopeful's hair stood out in all directions. It was so different from my sisters' straight hair that I stared at it.

Mrs. Mallone picked up the little crock and took off the top. She scooped up a mass of something smooth and reddish from inside that she rolled around with the tips of her fingers. She worked this into Hopeful's hair.

I'd never seen someone do that before, so I asked, "What's that?"

Mrs. Mallone laughed softly. "Palm tree oil. Hopeful's lucky, you know. Her papa can afford this. Some poor folks got nothing but drippings to treat their hair. Some don't even have that." She clucked her tongue. "Good Lord knows what we'll use for you once this runs out. Why did your papa drag us out here, heading farther from civilization every minute? Won't be able to get good palm tree oil in Kansas, I expect."

I was confused. My aunt had loved washing her hair in rainwater because she said it left her hair soft without being oily. And now here was Mrs. Mallone *adding* oil to Hopeful's hair. "What's it do?" I asked.

"Makes her hair behave. At least I can get some part of this girl to do things the way they ought."

Hopeful pressed her lips together.

I asked, "Do you put that palm tree stuff in your hair too?"

"Not often," she said. "I have better hair. Mine's almost straight and smooth without any help." She bent her head down, and I raised the lantern higher. "See? Almost as good as your sisters' hair."

"Is straight hair good?" I'd never thought this much about hair in my life, nor about whether there could be different kinds, good and bad. I'd always thought the curly red hair of the Barnes children on the next farm over had been the prettiest. But maybe curly hair was bad, and I didn't know it. Maybe girls and women knew this, but men didn't.

"Straight hair is more civilized," said Mrs. Mallone.

94

"Oh."

Hopeful spoke up at last, her voice soft. "Hair is hair."

"Don't mutter." Mrs. Mallone kept working the palm tree oil into Hopeful's hair, gradually easing out the tighter coils.

"White folks have straight hair, Levi," Hopeful explained. "White folks say it's better, and they've said it long enough and loud enough that they've gotten some black folks to believe it."

Mrs. Mallone's hands tightened in Hopeful's hair. "You think you know so much. You'll learn how much it matters. Straight hair *is* better."

Hopeful gritted her teeth. "It's just different. Not better."

Mrs. Mallone relaxed her fingers. "Can't teach this girl anything, Levi. Not a thing. Thinks she knows so much, growing up in the North and tasting freedom all her life. Straight hair gets you less attention. Takes less time to care for when you get worked so hard and long, you've hardly got time for sleep. My mama prayed for a baby with straight hair. Straight hair and light skin, and that's what she got. She wanted a better life for me. An easier life. Too bad your mama didn't pray for the same."

"Don't matter what you look like so much as what you do." Hopeful turned to me, drawing away from her stepmother. "You remember that, Levi. You learn that good."

"What you look like does matter," her stepmother argued. "You disgrace your papa and me when you dress like any old ragamuffin. You can't attract a good husband who'll provide you with a home if you look so unkempt." She clucked her tongue again. "It's too bad you're plain. I was married to my first man already by your age. And here you go about in those ugly dresses, your apron dirty, your hands rough as a washerwoman's."

I puzzled over that. I thought Hopeful was pretty. Not dazzling like Mrs. Mallone, but I recalled the times she'd smiled at me or the children. I thought of the way her face shone when she sang. How could her stepmother say she was plain?

Hopeful disagreed. "Some men value a woman for what she can do, not just how she looks. They like for a woman to know how to clean and cook. Some men want a woman who'll work alongside them."

Mrs. Mallone's fingers stilled, buried deep inside Hopeful's now-glossy hair. "I'm right, then."

"Right about what?"

Mrs. Mallone released Hopeful and reached for the brush. "You've been trying to catch that boy of Wallace's." She sank the brush in Hopeful's hair and yanked down, jerking Hopeful's head back. "He's nothing but a trailhand. A trailhand and a foundling, got no name of his own. Daughter of a preacher deserves better."

"Even if she's plain and has dirt on her hands?" Hopeful raised her head upright.

"You never do listen to my advice. I don't know why I bother." Mrs. Mallone continued brushing Hopeful's hair, though more gently.

Hopeful insisted, "Ness is going to be more than a trailhand. He and Wallace will be through leading wagon trains once they get us to Kansas."

"Oh, I heard all about that. About the house and ranchland Wallace owns, and him saving up for cattle. You really think he'll share it all with that foundling?" Mrs. Mallone teased out a knot in one lock of Hopeful's hair.

"Wallace says he couldn't run it without Ness." Hopeful sounded proud of them. "With what we're paying them, they'll have enough for fifty cows and a bull. Got the deal all fixed already with a cowman wanting to move to California."

Mrs. Mallone kept brushing. "I know. I'm pleased for them. But Wallace needs a good woman to settle him down. Man who's never married doesn't know how having a wife can be a comfort and a joy. Can build up his house and his land and make a real home. That's what any woman wants: a home with four walls and a good roof. Not a canvas roof, and not a cabin or a shack, but a house with a roof and a floor. And a man under it to care for. Men don't see the sense of that. They'll up and leave behind their comforts and travel around, build a shack someplace and live like peasants instead of like civilized folk. Someplace with no civilization. No stores, no schools, no churches, no nothing. What gets into a man to want that?"

Hopeful shrugged. "Don't know. Anyway, Wallace don't want a wife. Ness does."

"Ness don't know what he wants. Nor do you. Ranch or no ranch, I say the daughter of a preacher deserves better."

Hopeful turned to face her. "The daughter of a preacher? Or the wife of a preacher?" she asked, clear and bold.

Mrs. Mallone slapped her stepdaughter so hard Hopeful tipped off her stool sideways onto me. I staggered and nearly dropped the lantern. My own thoughts were as addled as if I'd been the one Mrs. Mallone had struck. All my idealized notions of her tilted out of alignment.

"How dare you?" Mrs. Mallone hissed. "How dare you say such a thing?"

"How dare you spend more time with Wallace than with my daddy?" Hopeful stood. "I've seen you with him. So has Ness. So have other people, I expect."

I recollected the hand-kissing and realized I was one of those people.

Mrs. Mallone spoke in her normal voice again. "You're imagining things. Wallace has been kind and attentive to all of us. Your papa leads these people, and Wallace works for him. Of course he spends more time with us than the others in the train."

Hopeful didn't reply.

"You been sleeping all right?" Mrs. Mallone asked her. "I could mix you something to help you sleep. Cure these wild ideas of yours."

"I sleep fine."

"Well, if you're sure." Mrs. Mallone gathered up the brush and her crock of palm tree oil, took the lantern from me, and mounted the steps to her wagon.

I turned away, but Hopeful reached out and took my arm. "Thank you," she whispered.

"For what?" I whispered back.

"For not leaving me alone with her." She gave my arm a squeeze, then hurried back to her tent without explaining any of what I'd witnessed.

I tried making sense of what the two women had said, but the conversation seemed to only touch on what they really meant. And that slap—I could still hear it, sharp and purposeful. I couldn't pretend she'd struck Hopeful by accident. Or that Hopeful had said anything that might deserve such a reaction from her stepmother.

I'd gotten whupped plenty by my parents when I

was younger, and my aunt and uncle too, if I'd been naughty. But there was a world of difference between that angry slap and the hiding a father gave a disobedient child. Because it didn't fit with my notions of Mrs. Mallone's beauty and goodness, it bothered me, and I resolved to push it out of my mind for the night and puzzle over it later.

I think back on my foolishness then and shake my head. I can see now that my confusion was a warning, some instinct inside me trying to get my attention. But right then, it only irritated me, an itch that I could not rid myself of.

CHAPTER TWELVE

The next morning brought me no answers, only more questions. When I took my turn at the water basin, washing the sleep out of my eyes before I started chores, I couldn't help but overhear an argument in the Mallone wagon. Canvas walls don't block much sound, and we'd all had to learn to ignore things said in the back of a neighboring wagon. So, I pretended not to hear.

But I heard.

"What would be wrong with that?" the Reverend Eli asked.

"It's just that she's young. And so's he, come to that." Mrs. Mallone's softer voice sounded soothing. "She's got no reason to see him again after this drive, and a girl needs to be careful."

"He's a good boy with a wide future ahead. He's honest and hardworking. If I had to pick a man for my daughter, I wouldn't find a better one."

"Well..." Mrs. Mallone let that word linger before continuing. "It's true she's got to move off on her own one day. Can't have her under my feet forever." She laughed a little. "But she hardly knows the boy. And I don't think Wallace wants him paying her so much attention."

"He's confided in you, has he? Wallace?"

"He doesn't have to. It's plain to see. But don't you worry, now. I didn't mean to start you fretting. I shouldn't have said a word. You got to rest peaceful and keep up your strength, after all."

"I'm feeling better this morning."

"Oh, that's good."

"Think I'll maybe step outside for a bit."

"That might not be wise. You don't want to get a chill. Sun's not up yet."

"Not that cold, is it? In May?"

"Colder than you might think. You stay right here. I'll bring you some breakfast."

I hustled over to the fire so I wouldn't get caught eavesdropping. I took my time pouring water into the coffee pot so that I was still there when Mrs. Mallone came over. Her skirts floated over the ground, she moved that elegantly. I'd just set the coffee pot back on the big rock beside the fire to get warm when the Reverend Eli left his wagon.

"Hopeful!" he said. "Wake up, child. I must speak

to you." Slowly, he climbed down the steps unaided.

Hopeful emerged from her tent all dressed for the day, her hair pinned up and tidy. "Morning, Daddy." She'd obviously been awake for some time. If I had heard all that discussion about her, she must have too.

"Hopeful, what is between you and young Ness?"

"Nothing," she answered, meeting his gaze.

"Lu says you two are mighty interested in each other."

Hopeful didn't look in her stepmother's direction. "Been talking to him. Making friends. He asked me to make him a promise, it's true. But I told him I can't leave you. Not with you feeling so poorly all the time now."

"What'd he say to that?"

"Didn't have time to say much at all. Wallace came over and told him to quit paying me notice when he should be working."

The Reverend Eli nodded twice, as if this settled everything. "And if I was to say it's time for you to make a home of your own? Would Ness be your choice?"

"I... I'm not ready to leave you."

"But if you were?" He glanced over at his wife, then back at Hopeful. "I'm not as strong as I used to be. This trip's been hard on me. I'm so weak some days, but still..."

"Trip won't be much longer." Hopeful took his hand. "You'll get well once we're settled."

"But if I don't, I'd want to know you had a good man like Ness."

"Then be at peace knowing good men live way out here too."

Mrs. Mallone returned to her husband's side. Her smile beamed bright and cheerful, but somehow strange, as though it masked some other emotion you wouldn't smile about. "You've set my mind at ease, child. How about you fix us some breakfast?"

"In a minute." Hopeful walked off toward those trees where she'd cried the day before. I wanted to follow her, but I knew if we weren't ready when Wallace said to leave, we risked getting left behind, so I set off about my morning tasks.

Jacob and I hitched up our teams while Laura and Martha got breakfast. Today, they remembered to cook extra for our noon meal. Lillie and the little boys stowed everything away. All around the ring of wagons, people bustled about, everyone busy with their own tasks.

As I buckled strap after strap of harness around one of our teams, Mrs. Mallone appeared beside me. I jumped, startling the horses. She could move quieter than a cat. I soothed them best I could. Last thing we needed was a bolting team half-hitched to our wagon.

Mrs. Mallone said, "I think your riding horse needs exercise. He seems restless."

Uncle Drew's horse twitched his ears, but looked peaceable, if alert. "Jacob rode him out hunting yesterday." I tried not to outright disagree with her.

"I could exercise him for you," she offered. "If I ride him this morning, it might settle him some."

"I'd have to ask Jacob," I mumbled. The horse belonged to him now, by rights.

"Really? You can't saddle him yourself? Oh. I see." She took a step away from me. "I'd just thought a ride might do me good as well. A bit of exercise might brighten me, but no matter."

Her disappointed frown troubled me. After her disagreement with her husband and Hopeful, of course she'd need some cheering up. How could I deny such a simple request? No doubt the horse would appreciate being away from all the dust.

Though I was bothered by her behavior toward Hopeful, I still couldn't bear to disoblige her if I could help it. "I can saddle him right enough. Do I have time? Wallace said to be ready to leave early and drive late."

"I'll see to it there's time."

"Wait here." I rushed to get Uncle Drew's saddle. I'd almost finished cinching the girth when Jacob came around the corner of the wagon.

"What're you doing?" he demanded.

"Mrs. Mallone offered to exercise him."

"Why?"

"Any reason why she shouldn't?"

"He ain't yours to loan out, for one thing."

"I don't see how that matters! I'm the one that has to brush him and water him and picket him and... and everything! You walk around like you're a grown-up now, but you expect me to do all the work. And I'm tired of it, Jacob!" Which was not at all what I'd meant to say when I'd first started talking, but the words sort of took hold of me and kept coming, with or without my say-so.

"Anything else?"

"You bet! I'm nearly as growed as you are, and I'm tired of you treating me same as Henry or Caleb."

Jacob put his fists on his hips. "Is that so? Well, let me tell you something, Levi. You'll do as I tell you, or you can clear out! I'm doing everything I can to get us to Uncle Matthew all in one piece. Until we find him, I hold that responsibility, you hear? But if you don't want to string along with me, then you can go. You take that horse and whatever food you can scrounge up, and you go be a big man on your own with no one telling you what to do."

"You don't mean that." My voice cracked. Jacob and I'd had our differences for years, but I'd never thought he wanted to be rid of me.

"I do mean it! You can light out for Texas or California or... or the devil!"

Before I could reply, he stomped away.

I didn't want to leave. I only wanted to let Mrs. Mallone ride Uncle Drew's horse. Sure, I was tired of Jacob bossing me, but I'd had no thought of leaving. Miserably, I decided to ignore what he'd said and drive my wagon like always.

I led the horse to her. "Hold him so I can mount," she told me, and I obliged. She rode away without thanking me.

When Ness loped his big bay down the outside of the ring letting us know it was time to go, I clambered up to my own seat.

"Lead them out, Miss Mallone." Ness wheeled his mount and sped past me, on up the road. He sounded curt, even cold. Hopeful had obviously told her father the truth, that Ness and she had parted badly. What a mess people made of each other's feelings sometimes, I thought in all my fourteen-year-old wisdom.

Wallace rode on ahead of the train as usual. Beside him on Uncle Drew's horse, Mrs. Mallone smiled at the world. But mostly at Wallace.

I didn't want that to bother me. I didn't want to be bothered by the Reverend Eli and his wife having an argument, nor by Hopeful's accusing words. Nor by that slap.

But my mind wouldn't dwell on anything else all morning. I puzzled over it all while I kept my horses following in the hoofprints of thousands upon thousands of other animals that had drawn endless wagonloads of hopes and dreams and problems and worries, hauling them west, west, always west.

CHAPTER THIRTEEN

Dusk closed around us before Wallace gave the order to make camp that evening. Folks grumbled, but from what I could gather from their mutterings, a longer day on the trail Monday was how Wallace always made up a little for stopping all day Sunday. By the time we'd picketed the horses, the first stars had come out. I was glad for their light, but still stumbled over half-seen obstacles on my way to the campfire and a late supper. Jacob spoke not a single word to me that whole day, though I couldn't tell if he ignored me because he was annoyed I'd stayed or embarrassed over our argument.

Mrs. Mallone had ridden Uncle Drew's saddle horse all day. I'd not seen her at our noon stop. Stuck in our usual place at the tail end of the train, I hadn't seen much in front of me but the back of Jacob's wagon. That meant I didn't know until evening that she'd accompanied Wallace on his scouting ahead, leaving Ness with the train in case of trouble.

I learned that from Laura after supper. She told me Mrs. Mallone seemed a fine rider, but that's about all she would say. She'd walked beside Hopeful much of the day. Laura was full of things Hopeful had told her about growing up in Ohio, the daughter of a respected preacher. "Hopeful says they had a house with six rooms, can you imagine? Upstairs, they had her bedroom, her parents' room, and a guest room, too. And they had a kitchen, a parlor, and a sitting room for everyday down below. A big garden and apple orchard out back. And a porch in front. You think the house Uncle Matthew is building for us has a porch?"

I didn't often let myself think about what would happen after we found Uncle Matthew. "Maybe."

"Hopeful's ma died when she was real young, but so many ladies from the church took good care of her that she never noticed the lack. Her pa never acted interested in getting married again until Mrs. Mallone moved there from Louisiana three years back. Her first husband died, I guess, and she sold his feed store or something and moved up north. And next thing Hopeful knew, everybody kept telling her how lucky she was to have a ma. But I don't think she likes her stepmother, do you?"

I didn't want to answer that directly. I'd maybe have to admit that Mrs. Mallone had struck her, and Hopeful had practically said she feared her. So, I searched for a way to excuse both of them. "Maybe she's jealous. Doesn't like sharing her pa's time. You know, like when Lillie was born."

"Lillie?"

"You were just two, so you don't remember, I expect. You didn't want to share Ma's lap with her. You called her 'that baby' for the longest time."

"I did?" Laura's voice got quiet. "Caleb didn't do that with baby Andrew. Why did I?"

"Caleb was three, not two. And Caleb had been sharing Aunt Phoebe with all of us already. Maybe that's why."

"Maybe." Laura sat beside me in silence for some time. Finally, she said, "No, Hopeful doesn't sound jealous. And they got married years ago already— you'd think she'd have had time to get used to things. I think it's something different."

"Maybe she's afraid of her."

"What?"

I backtracked some. "Afraid of displeasing her, I mean. Mrs. Mallone is so, well, lovely and ladylike, and Hopeful's more..." I searched for a word.

"Natural?"

"Could be." I shifted the conversation. "How come they're leaving their six-room house with a porch?"

"Lot of folks in their church moved to Ohio from Tennessee, after the war I guess. They got word a lot of family and friends back in Tennessee meant to move to Kansas and find a better life. Same as us. These folks decided to go west too, with the others, and they asked the Reverend Eli to organize things and guide them and start a church there. Hopeful says she was glad to come, and the Reverend too, but I think Mrs. Mallone wasn't. Hopeful said she cried every day for a week over leaving."

"She's not crying now."

"No."

No. Now, it was Hopeful who'd cried alone among the trees, as if she and her stepmother had traded griefs.

Henry and Caleb fell asleep with their supper half-eaten. I gobbled up their leftover cornbread and salt pork while the girls bundled the little ones into their beds. I never got enough to eat, according to my innards, and the extra mouthfuls were welcome.

Hopeful watched me cleaning their plates. "Still hungry?"

"Ain't it bad manners to say yes when the food's gone anyway?"

"I won't tell. Want an apple? We still got lots of those."

"Yes, please."

"An apple it is, then." She headed for her wagon, leaving me alone beside the fire, for Jacob had gone to check the horses.

Mrs. Mallone had taken supper to her husband in his bed, then eaten her own elsewhere. Now, she approached her wagon just as Hopeful opened the flap and came out.

"What are you doing in there?" Mrs. Mallone demanded.

Hopeful didn't respond.

"What are you doing?" Mrs. Mallone grabbed her wrist. "Answer me!"

"I'm getting Levi an apple." Hopeful held up her free hand, showing her the fruit. "Why shouldn't I go in my own wagon where my daddy is sleeping?"

Mrs. Mallone let go of her. "I—I don't want your papa disturbed."

Hopeful raised her other hand. "Or were you worried I'd find this?"

From my seat by the fire, I couldn't see exactly what she held, but it glinted in the flickering light like glass.

"Where did you get that?" Mrs. Mallone grabbed for the object, but Hopeful held it out of reach.

"It's laudanum, isn't it?" Hopeful asked.

"It helps your papa sleep. He was restless. It's dangerous, and I need to put it away. I didn't realize

I'd left it out. Give it to me!" Mrs. Mallone held out her hand, insistent, commanding.

"It's almost empty. Wasn't it near full last week when you gave Delia some for her headache?"

"No, it wasn't. Give it to me. That's expensive, and who knows if I'll be able to get more tomorrow."

"Tomorrow?"

"We reach Independence tomorrow. Early, maybe mid-morning. We'll have time to pick up supplies and maybe even cross the river, Wallace says."

"I see." Hopeful dropped the glass bottle into her stepmother's waiting hand. "Wallace says. Wallace, Wallace, Wallace. I think I really do see. At last."

Mrs. Mallone slipped the bottle into a pocket in her skirt. "What do you see?"

"I see so much I could—"

Mrs. Mallone grabbed both of Hopeful's arms and shook her until her head wobbled. "No, you see nothing," she hissed. "You hear me? Nothing. And anything you think you know, you can't—"

"Prove?" Hopeful laughed a hard, mocking laugh. "Of course not."

"Just you remember that." Mrs. Mallone pushed her to the side and disappeared into her wagon.

Hopeful handed me the apple. "Have you seen Ness?"

"Not since this morning. What's laudanum?"

"It makes you sleep. I've got to talk to Ness. If

you see him, tell him I'm looking for him. I'll meet him out where he picketed our horses." She hurried away, leaving me with my apple and my questions. I was having a harder and harder job pushing those questions away and reminding myself Mrs. Mallone was a good, kind healer.

The next day rolled along the same as the one before, at the beginning. I fetched an extra bucket of water for Mrs. Mallone while Jacob carried ours. I hoped that, when I brought her the water, I could ask her to teach me more about herbs and remedies and healing folks. Even show me her medicine chest again, maybe tell me about just one thing in it. Maybe explain what that laudanum stuff was. She'd said she'd teach me in the evenings but, so far, her evenings had been filled with one thing or another, never lessons in healing.

Her arguments with Hopeful troubled me. I'd not seen Ness, and Hopeful's eyes were rimmed in red that morning, like she'd been crying. But I lied to myself, saying this was none of my business. Mrs. Mallone must have her stepdaughter's best interests in mind, and her husband's too. She must have her reasons for treating Hopeful kind one day, then angry and even mean the next. I told myself I couldn't know better than a grown woman about how to behave.

When I got back from the nearby pond, Mrs. Mallone stood behind her wagon, waiting for me. She took a looking glass from the pocket of her skirt. A hand mirror so elegant and fancied up, I stared at it instead of her.

I'd seen looking glasses before. My mother had had one, and my Aunt Phoebe. Both were packed somewhere in our trunks, though my mother's had cracked diagonally across its face.

It wasn't the polished surface reflecting Mrs. Mallone's loveliness that I marveled at, but the filigreed metal that held it. Ma's mirror had a simple metal frame with her initials etched on the back. Aunt Phoebe's was fancier, with violets painted on its porcelain back, and it had a brush that matched.

But Mrs. Mallone's looking glass was a work of art. Nothing else you could call it. Vines and flowers twined all around the mirror's surface and down around the handle. The back of the mirror had a tree engraved on it, framed with those vines and flowers. I tried identifying the tree by its general shape, but Mrs. Mallone lowered it before I had a chance.

"You've never seen anything like this, have you."

"No, ma'am."

"Ever look in a mirror?"

"Not of late."

Mrs. Mallone turned the reflecting side toward

me. "You're not such a bad-looking boy. Might even grow neat and respectable."

I set down the water bucket and studied my reflection. My ears stuck out more than I'd recalled. And my brown hair had grown long, brushing over my eyebrows. Aunt Phoebe would've cut it by now. I pushed it back. Couldn't hide those ears.

"Mirrors never lie," Mrs. Mallone told me. "Good and bad, happy and sad, they show what's truly there. Nothing more and nothing less. You can fool people, but you can't fool a mirror." She looked past me. "Isn't that so?" she asked someone behind me.

Hopeful came over bearing a bowl of cornmeal mush for her father. "If you say it's so, it must be so." She climbed up to the back of their wagon.

Mrs. Mallone turned the mirror back around and smiled at her own reflection. She paid no more heed to me. I left, my questions about remedies unasked.

As before, I waited with my wagon behind Jacob until all the others had filed past. We took our places at the end of the line, but I didn't mind the dust so much for once. Today, we'd reach Independence, that fabled "jumping off place" where the great wagon trains of the past had made their start. Years earlier, those making for new homes in Oregon or California had gathered there, forming trains as long as five miles, I'd heard.

But I looked forward to Independence for a different reason. Jacob intended to send a telegram to Uncle Matthew from there. We'd inform him that Uncle Drew and Aunt Phoebe and baby Andrew had left us, and that we were coming ahead anyhow. Jacob hadn't told me that directly, as he continued to ignore me. But he'd told the girls in my hearing, and that was good enough.

Somehow, it heartened me to know my only remaining adult kin would learn of our plight and be expecting us. Might even ride out and meet us. We'd originally planned to find a wagon train of white folks in Independence we could join up with, but I guess we'd gotten attached to the people in this train. Even if most of the colored people ignored us still, enough acted friendly to make us feel a little welcome. Jacob meant to ask Wallace if we could continue on with them until our uncle met up with us.

I drove my team those last few miles with something close to hope in my heart. By the end of the day, we'd be across the Missouri River, the final barrier between us and Kansas and our new lives.

CHAPTER FOURTEEN

Independence held so many buildings, I gave up counting them. After jolting over a set of railroad tracks, we halted. Before us lay the brown, seething river. Spring rains had fed it until it seemed about to burst its banks like a fat man's shirtfront. It made all the other rivers we'd forded or been ferried across look tame.

Wallace rode down the line of wagons, talking with drivers as he passed them. I set my brake and waited for Wallace or Jacob to tell me what to do next. My sisters and little cousins gathered nearby.

Jacob looped his reins around the brake handle and climbed down. For the first time in days, he spoke directly to me. "Wallace says we'll all wait here for our turn on the ferry. Ness went ahead to make the arrangements already. I asked Wallace where the telegraph office is, and he said to look for the train

119

depot, and there'll be one there. Says we can buy anything we need at the stores in town. He and Ness and a few others will stay with the wagons to guard our belongings."

"I'm ready." I secured my own reins around my brake and jumped down. Jacob and I watered our horses with buckets and hooked feedbags over their noses so they could eat while we were in town.

All seven of us tramped into Independence, little Henry and Caleb holding Laura and Martha's hands. We gawked at the buildings, how many there were and how big they all looked. I counted four church towers at varying distances from us.

The train depot was somewhat removed from the bulk of the city. I waited outside with the younger children when Jacob went inside. He insisted one almost-grown person would attract less attention than seven kids with no adults. We knew that we could be in a sort of danger from any passing busybodies or do-gooders who might decide they should "rescue" us. If anyone asked what we were doing, I'd say we were waiting there for our folks. That wouldn't even be a lie, for we were waiting for Jacob, and he was some of our kinfolk.

So, we waited, bright May sunshine warming us until we crowded into the scanty shade of the depot's eaves. Noon edged close, and I knew I wasn't the only one hungry. Trying to keep Henry and Caleb from fussing made the wait stretch longer and longer.

The station was busy, people coming and going, buying tickets or inquiring about trains and so forth. It struck me that almost everyone we saw now had white skin like us. In only a couple of days, I'd grown used to seeing faces of all different shades, but now the only skin darker than my own belonged to two men stacking crates beside the station platform. They kept their eyes down, paying no mind to anyone. I realized it might be best if I did the same. No sense drawing attention to us by staring at people.

All we wanted was to go find Uncle Matthew, though we had no real acquaintance with him. When he'd left for the west, I'd only been six years old. I had only one sliver of a memory of him, that he wore tall black boots. Cavalry boots, Pa had called them. I'd loved staring at them, shiny and utterly different from Pa's patched and rough work boots. My sisters didn't remember him at all.

Near-stranger or no, Uncle Matthew was our goal, our destination, our hope.

Finally, Jacob led us into Independence. We bought bread, ham, and a big wedge of cheese and ate them squatting in the shade of a tree along a dusty side street. After our trail rations of mainly cornbread, salt pork, and sometimes venison, the bread and cheese were a particular treat. Henry and Caleb ate until they looked sick.

Sending that telegram to Uncle Matthew had relieved Jacob's mind, I could tell. He smiled at his siblings twice on the way to find food. Buying our noon meal had been his idea, a way of celebrating. Only a hundred and some miles to Junction City, where Uncle Matthew would likely meet us. Why, we might even be there by the end of the week!

As much of a treat as the bread and cheese were, we enjoyed one purchase even more: milk fresh from a cow that morning. Uncle Drew had sold his two cows and their calves before we left. A few folks in this wagon train had milk cows, but we never dared ask them to share. Plenty of little ones of their own needing it, and we'd done without it before anyhow. Jacob claimed he bought this milk for Henry and Caleb, but we all enjoyed swigging from the glass bottles.

I leaned back and gazed at the sky. Lazy clouds drifted by, and I wished I could let my thoughts drift off along with them. Maybe even fall asleep there, half in shade, half in sunshine.

"What're you thinking on so hard, Levi?" Lillie asked me.

"I'm looking forward," I said, slow and sleepy.

"To what?"

"Just forward. Instead of back." I didn't know how to explain myself better than that. For so long, I'd looked away from my future. Back to my parents, after they passed on. Back to Uncle Drew and Aunt Phoebe's home after they sold it and headed west. Back to their graves after they died too. But now, I found myself looking forward, toward something coming up instead of back at where I'd already been.

An uncle who wore tall black boots might not be much to fix your hopes on, but it's what I had. It was enough. It had to be.

"You mean forward to meeting Uncle Matthew?" Lillie asked, soft and worried.

"Yeah. Aren't you?"

"I wish we were there already. I keep thinking, who'll die next? But then I think, if we can all get to Uncle Matthew, somehow, we'll be safe. Won't we?"

I sat up and pulled my littlest sister close. We sat together, my arm around her shoulders, her cheek resting on my arm. I'd gotten wrapped up in my own thoughts and ideas and problems, and I'd ignored Lillie and Laura. Left them to mind Henry and Caleb and keep Martha company. I saw then that I'd held myself away from them.

I didn't know what to say. Who'll die next? I'd avoided that question ever since we left those two graves along the trail. It had driven me to ask Mrs.

Mallone to teach me something about healing folks, made me dream of becoming a doctor someday. I needed to learn how to keep people from dying. "We'll be there soon," I told her. "Just a few more days. Won't be long at all."

When we'd all finished, Laura and Martha picked up the milk bottles and the scattered bits of greased paper that the cheese and ham had come wrapped in. Jacob planned to stop at a feed and grain store to buy oats for our horses. Laura wanted to find a dry goods store to see if anyone was selling eggs. Lillie asked if we could see about other sundries there, though she didn't say exactly what, and I figured she had her mind on stick candy.

Jacob must have figured the same thing. First mercantile we found, he told me to wait outside with the younger ones while he and Laura went in. Laura came out hugging a bag of coffee beans, for ours were running low. Jacob had a crate containing a whole dozen precious eggs. One each for us for breakfast, and five to bake with, Laura said.

And tucked in the corner of Jacob's crate was a small brown paper bag. "Take the bag, will you, Martha?" Jacob said casually.

Martha obediently took the bag and peeked inside. "Peppermints!" she breathed, joy shining in her wide eyes. "So many peppermints, Jacob!"

We stared at her. They were the first real words

she'd spoken since her parents died, aside from singing by their graves.

Martha seemed not to notice our stares, but joyfully doled out the candy, one for each of us. She tucked the bag of leftovers in her apron pocket, and we all sucked the sweet, round peppermints as we continued down the sidewalk. Not one of us had thought to thank Jacob, but our contented smiles showed our gratitude clear enough. I could hear Henry crunching his already, grinding it between those tiny teeth of his.

As we headed for a feed store Jacob remembered passing on our way into town, who should we see but Wallace and Hopeful. They stood beside a three-story building marked "Rooms to Let." Hopeful's folded arms and the way she shook her head over and over made it plain she disagreed with every word Wallace said. He towered over her, shaking his finger in her face.

We all stopped so suddenly, Martha bumped into Caleb, knocking him to his hands and knees. His peppermint popped out of his mouth, hit the wooden sidewalk, and broke. He wailed.

Hopeful and Wallace both looked over at us, and Wallace stepped back. Under his black horseshoe mustache, his lips made a stern line.

Jacob walked up to them, though the rest of us stayed back. "Is it time for us to drive out to the ferry?" he asked, his voice as calm as if he was passing the time of day. He kept going until he stood slightly in front of Hopeful. Like a shield. Or a knight. Like he was protecting her.

Wallace crossed his arms over his chest, mirroring Hopeful. "Yes."

"Good." Jacob turned to Hopeful then. "Can we escort you back to your pa's wagon?" He offered her his arm like a real gentleman, best he could while carrying the egg crate. I saw him in a new way, saw he was almost a man grown, and a good man at that. It never occurred to me then, but I see now how hard it must have been for my cousin, suddenly caring for six youngsters. It had made him grow up all at once. No wonder he'd gotten so bossy.

Hopeful's voice faltered. "Thank you, Jacob, but I'm not... I'm not coming."

"Oh?" Jacob looked Wallace in the eye. "Why not?"

"Miss Mallone is no longer welcome in our train."

"Has she done something wrong, Mr. Wallace? There some reason she can't keep traveling along with you?"

"I'm the wagon master. What I say goes. I say who gets to go and who don't."

"That's not a real reason."

"That's all you're getting."

"I see." Jacob took a deep breath. "Mr. Wallace,

we won't be continuing on with you either. We'll stay here with Miss Mallone until she's settled."

"As you like."

Hopeful glared at Wallace. "She put you up to this, didn't she. She told you to get rid of me."

Wallace didn't meet her gaze. "I make my own decisions, Miss Mallone. And what I say goes, you know that."

"She lets you think so. I see things too, Wallace. I see more than I want to. I need to get back to the wagons."

"You stay here," Wallace insisted. "Don't follow us. And don't think you can tempt my boy away from me, either."

Hopeful's eyes filled with tears. "I never would have," she said, her voice choked and shaky. "May I say goodbye to my daddy, at least?"

"He's already crossed the river. All the wagons have, except their two." He jerked a thumb at us.

"You're abandoning me?" Her voice quavered again. "What will I do?"

"Maybe you can keep house for these seven white children you're so fond of." With that, he spun on his heel and crossed the street. The rest of us crowded around Hopeful and Jacob.

Hopeful sank down on a wooden box. "How can he do this?" she murmured. "My daddy... he's been too sick..." She twisted her hands in her apron, bunching it up without noticing what she did. "And I think she's... she's trying to..."

Jacob dropped to his heels beside her. "You're coming with us." He put a hand over hers to still them. "We'll follow them. No law against that."

"But Wallace said not to. What will happen to all of you if he finds out?"

"Your pa loves you, Hopeful. Everyone knows that. And I've seen Wallace bow to the Reverend's wishes, haven't you? If your pa says you can stay with him, what can Wallace do?"

"It's not Wallace's doing, not really. It's her. My stepmother."

I wanted to jump to Mrs. Mallone's defense. I wanted to ask Hopeful how she could say that when her stepmother took such good care of her father. I wanted to point out the way Mrs. Mallone doctored everyone else in the wagon train and kept them from dying of fevers. But somehow, I couldn't find the right words. Instead of Mrs. Mallone's beautiful face and soft voice, I saw her slapping Hopeful. Arguing with the Reverend Eli. Whispering with Wallace.

I tried anyway. "Surely Wallace is just angry because of you and Ness being..."

Laura clamped her hand over my mouth. "Don't mind him," she told Hopeful. "He never knows when to hush. You come with us. We'll find your pa again, don't you worry. And Ness too, I'm sure."

Hopeful closed her eyes and leaned her head back against the wall. "Please, Jesus, let me not be too late." She opened her eyes and stood up. "Let's go, then. Time's a-wasting."

CHAPTER FIFTEEN

When we returned to our wagons, we got a surprise. And not the nice kind, either. Someone had unhitched both our teams and staked them out in the paltry grass nearby, then dumped the harnesses in a pile in the back of the wagons. I could see they were so tangled up, we'd have to sort them out before we could hitch up the teams. Someone sure-enough knew how to delay people.

Jacob said, "Let the teams graze. The rest of you can stay here, and I'll ride down to the river and see how much the ferry costs. Maybe find a wagon train willing to take us on until we can catch up with the others." He climbed in the wagon he usually drove and rustled around. I knew he was getting money for the ferry, and maybe for a new wagon master too. I clambered up and tried making sense of the mess of straps and buckles we had to untangle.

Jacob saddled up the riding horse and rode away before I had one set of reins free. It would be a long, weary chore. Laura got the little ones playing "Ring Around the Rosy" to keep them occupied and out of the harnesses.

Hopeful climbed up beside me to help. Thanks to her, it didn't take as long to sort out two full pairs of harness as I'd feared. Hopeful didn't speak more than a dozen words the whole time. I kept silent too, not knowing what to say. How would you comfort a person who's been cast out of their family and left behind by everyone they know? Or, almost everyone.

It must be almost like having your parents die, I realized. Except Hopeful had no kin to share the pain of this separation. She only had us.

Jacob rode up in a whirl of dust. "Let's go! Let's go! If we can get to the ferry before sundown, we can cross today yet!"

We hustled to hitch up the teams. Hopeful helped right alongside me. The determined way she buckled those straps told me she would do anything possible to get herself and us across that river before nightfall. To get that much closer to her father again.

The ferry landing was awfully noisy. Horses, mules, dogs, and oxen voiced their distaste for waiting, men and women shouted at their animals, and children added fractious end-of-day howls to the din. But we eventually drove our wagons onto the wooden ferry as though we'd crossed rivers on rafts all our lives instead of only a couple times before. I hated crossing on ferries. They always looked flimsy and prone to sinking.

When our wheels touched solid ground again, Jacob led the way until we reached a wagon train circled not far off the road. The sight of all those wagons together was like seeing home again after a long journey. If I'd let myself, I would've cried. They weren't *our* train, but the circle of wagons looked familiar and safe anyhow.

Jacob drove toward them, and I figured we would ask if we could join them for the night instead of camping all by ourselves. Thieves liked preying on lone wagons, especially at night, or so Uncle Drew had told us. He'd worried a whole lot about that when our train left us behind on account of their sickness.

I realized then that we'd done it. We had reached Kansas at last. I'd expected to feel more excited. More relieved. Maybe happy. But all I felt was tired.

Jacob halted his team facing the circle, and I pulled up alongside. Jacob addressed the curious people watching us. "There a man here named Hauer?"

No one answered him.

"They told me your wagon master was named Hauer. Isn't that so?" Jacob asked.

A man pushed his way through the crowd. Tall, lean, and with a reddish beard cut close to his jaw, he wore beechnut homespun trousers, a grimy red shirt, and a gray hat with yellow tassels.

"Yes, that's so," the man acknowledged around the cigar clamped between his teeth.

"Are you Hauer?"

"No."

"Where is he? I need to talk with him."

"He ain't here just now. Whatcha need, boy?" he drawled, slow and deliberate, stretching the middles of the words until they contained more sounds than I was used to.

"I need a place for us to stay for the night. We got left behind, and we'll be on our way in the morning to catch up with our wagon train. The man at the ferry said to find Hauer, that he'd help."

The man took his cigar from his mouth and spat on the ground. "What train was you with? Only one that I seen pass us was a bunch of darkies. Yours must've been long gone before you noticed. Where's your pa? Let me speak with him."

Jacob said, clear and firm, "My pa died, and my ma too. I'm in charge of us."

The man laughed a braying, mocking laugh. "Are you now? Good for you, son. How many of you is there?"

"I don't see how that signifies. We won't bother anybody. We only want to camp with you for the one night."

"Afraid of wolves, I take it?" The man chuckled. "Trouble is, we're all unhitched. Can't move those wagons by snapping our fingers, can we? But I tell you what, you can pull up alongside us, and you can sleep inside the circle if you want. That satisfy you?"

Jacob shrugged. "Thanks, I guess. That'll have to do."

I swung my team to the right and drove it farther up, giving Jacob room to do the same. We unhitched in the waning light while Hopeful and the girls brought some cooking things out. Laura and Martha slipped between the wagons near us to reach the cooking fires inside. But Hopeful hung back with Lillie and the little boys, quietly telling them a story to keep them from wandering off.

Jacob and I were coming back from watering and staking out the horses when we heard the man Jacob had parleyed with earlier say, "Well, what have we here? These kids got themselves a darky for a nursemaid!" He laughed unpleasantly again. "Must be your pa left you pretty well off if you can afford that. Darkies don't work cheap these days."

Jacob and I found the grey-hatted man leaning against one of our wagons, sneering at Hopeful. My sisters and cousins crowded around her, but stayed behind her too.

Hopeful had her fists on her hips, her chin high. "We earn our pay."

The man pulled his cigar from between his lips and aimed the soggy end at her. "Don't mouth off to me, girl, or I'll learn you some manners. You best remember your place."

Jacob came forward. "Her place is here with us. But yours isn't." He stood beside Hopeful, in front of the little ones. "You mind your own business, and we'll mind ours."

Once again, I found myself filled with admiration for Jacob and the way he stood up to another adult I would be scared to speak to at all. I remembered what Hopeful had said about him needing time to find himself. Maybe this was what she'd meant. That Jacob would find a grown-up version of himself somewhere along the trail.

"Or what?" The man made a big show of looking Jacob up and down.

"Or we'll camp someplace else."

"Who's stopping you?"

A new voice came out of the dusk. "I am." A man walked toward us leading a small horse, almost a pony, dark brown with a spread of white over its rump behind the man's saddle. It was the first I'd seen of what they call an Indian pony or Appaloosa.

Next to such a striking horse, the man seemed downright ordinary. He wore his battered hat pushed back off his forehead, his gun belt strapped snug around his waist. His fringed buckskin coat was missing about half of its fringe. He could've been anyone at all, or nobody, one of a hundred men I'd seen dressed just the same.

But his serious face had an openness that made me think I could get to liking him. Maybe it was how his eyes crinkled at the sides, as if he smiled a good deal. Maybe it was my relief at an adult stepping in to help us.

"I couldn't help overhearing," this man said. "I'm sorry I wasn't on hand when you arrived. I'm Hauer." He shook hands with Jacob, ignoring the man with the cigar.

"Jacob Dalton. This is Miss Mallone."

"Pleased to know you." Hauer shook hands with Hopeful as well. "If you folks want to camp with us, we'll widen the circle in no time." He raised his voice to reach the people inside the camp. "I know there's plenty of good, strong men here who can swing these wagons out some."

The man with the cigar glared at Hauer. He stood a good bit taller than the wagon master, but Hauer seemed to look down at him somehow.

"Something on your mind, Sanderson?" Hauer asked quietly.

"No," Sanderson said around his cigar. "Not a thing." He stalked away, long legs in pale brown trousers slicing the air like a pair of scissors.

CHAPTER SIXTEEN

I woke in the grayness of too-early morning, my mind fuzzy. It took me several seconds to blink some sense into my brain. What had tugged me out of my sleep? I lay still and listened. Nothing in the wagon above me made a sound.

Then I heard noise and knew it for what it was: footsteps in the grass outside the circle. Cautious, steady footsteps approaching the wagon Jacob slept under.

Thieves! Thieves after our money, just how Jacob had said. And Hopeful was sleeping in that wagon—thieves might kill her to get the money.

How could I wake Jacob and Hopeful without alerting the thief? I couldn't call out, not even a whisper. If I did, a thief would surely knife me to keep me quiet. I risked turning my head and saw a pair of legs in dark pants coming from the direction of the road. A horse followed the man, close.

Then out of the dark came another pair of legs, these ones in lighter-colored trousers, moving fast. "Hold it, boy!" said a voice I remembered only too well from a few hours earlier.

The first man stopped mid-step. "Easy, Mister," said Ness's familiar voice, soft but distinct.

I rolled out from under my wagon. "Ness!" I half-whispered. "You're—" I stopped, my words forgotten, for Sanderson had a double-barreled shotgun aimed at Ness.

"I see how it is," Sanderson said. "Send the kids in to size up the camp, and then they can tell you where to find the cash boxes and the best horses."

"You got this all wrong." Ness raised his hands high. He held his reins in one fist, his big bay horse close beside him, and he let the reins slide through his fingers until he grasped them near his horse's head.

"Don't you argue with me! I got no patience for uppity darkies." Sanderson stepped closer until he could jam the muzzle of his shotgun into Ness's midsection.

"Please," I begged, "don't shoot. I know him. He's from the wagon train we were with." I stumbled toward them, shaking, but forcing myself to keep moving, keep talking extra-loud. Hoping someone would wake up and come stop this. "They must've realized we got left behind. Isn't that so, Ness? And you come looking for us?"

"I been looking all night for you."

Behind me, I heard one of our wagons creak and shift from someone climbing out of it. Then Hopeful said, "There you are, Ness. I knew it'd be you that came back for us. Are the others camped near? If we hurry, we can catch up this morning." She walked over to stand beside me. Her words floated clear and loud in the morning air, and I knew she hoped to waken others in the camp, same as I'd tried to do.

Ness glanced at Hopeful. "They're not far, no."

"Likely story," sneered Sanderson.

Where was Jacob? Why didn't he come out here and back up what we said? Surely he couldn't be sleeping through all this.

"If we wanted to rob you, why do it now?" Hopeful asked. "Why not farther up the trail, away from the city? Independence has law and order. Only a fool would commit a crime this close by."

"I got no notion how a thief's mind works," Sanderson said. "Nor no darky's neither. I only know I caught me one sneaking around in the dead of night. Can't tell me you ain't up to something you got no right to be."

I prayed silently for the Lord to send Hauer, send Jacob, send anyone at all who would help.

Ness said slowly, "Are you calling me a liar?"

"I'll call you anything I want." Sanderson shoved Ness with the end of his shotgun hard enough to push Ness back a step.

What happened next was a blur in the vague pre-dawn dimness. Ness smashed his free hand into the shotgun so it pointed at the ground. At the same time, he yanked his horse's head forward and down in front of him.

The horse neighed in Sanderson's face right as the shotgun went off, both barrels. The blast of that gun kicked grass and dirt high in the air, making it even harder to see what happened. My ears rang from the noise. Bits of dirt and grass pelted me as they fell, prickling all over my face and arms.

Then Ness had the shotgun aiming straight up between him and Sanderson. In camp, a woman screamed. Several little ones cried. Men shouted and yelled, but the noise of that gunshot addled my hearing so I couldn't make out words, only sounds all muffled and jumbled.

Ness broke open the shotgun and ejected its shells. He'd dropped his horse's reins, and it bolted toward the road. Ness threw the shotgun away from him and kept facing Sanderson, who had retreated a few paces.

Hopeful took two hesitant steps, then ran to Ness. She put both her arms around his waist and pressed her cheek against his shoulder. Ness kept his right hand free, hanging low near the pistol he wore. But his left arm crushed Hopeful to him.

From behind me, men came running. I shook my head, their voices still a rattling buzz in my ears. Then Jacob was there, shaking me and talking.

"I can't hear you." My voice wavered. Tears built up behind my eyes. "I can't hear you, Jacob. I don't know what you want."

Jacob surprised me. He put his arms around my shoulders and hugged me close as though I was one of his own siblings. I could feel his voice vibrating in his chest, could hear he was talking, but I couldn't make sense of the words yet. But I didn't need to.

When Jacob let me go, I saw Hauer and two other men standing in a triangle around Sanderson. Hauer had his hand on his own holstered pistol, and he looked plenty upset. I stuck my fingers in my ears and wiggled them. I could make out some words now, though a loud ringing jangled constantly under the other sounds.

Jacob was telling me, "...to fetch Hauer as fast as I could, but we were too late. And when I heard that shotgun, Levi, I feared... I feared too many things."

"Me too." I watched Hauer and Sanderson as they exchanged angry words. I had a hard time thinking past the fact that I'd been that close to seeing another person die. Die in such a different way from my ma and pa, aunt and uncle and baby cousin. I started shaking then, and Jacob led me back inside the circle of wagons.

Jacob sat me down beside Ness and Hopeful on a blanket near the cookfire we'd shared with others the night before. My sisters and cousins tumbled out of the wagon, staring and questioning and getting in Jacob's way. He dragged two more blankets out, gave one to Ness and Hopeful, and wrapped the other around me. I didn't know why I was shivering, for the night hadn't been a cold one. But I filled with so much gratitude for that blanket, tears ran down my cheeks. I was glad dawn had barely begun unrolling over us, for maybe no one saw my crying.

Jacob and my sisters stoked up the fire until they had a cheery blaze. Laura put water for coffee over the fire to heat, and I realized the ringing in my ears had lessened some already.

Hauer and the other men entered the circle, Hauer holding the empty shotgun. Two men held Sanderson between them, each gripping one of his arms. Hauer stopped them a little way from our campfire. "All right," the wagon master said, "I want to hear what happened. All of it. First from you." He nodded to Ness.

"Why him first?" Sanderson protested.

"He's the one who almost got shot," Hauer said. To Ness, he added, "I don't guess I know your name. Mine's Hauer." He held out his hand.

Ness stood up. He eyed Hauer's hand warily before he shook it. "Ness. Onesimus Wallace, if you want my entitles."

"Mr. Wallace, good to meet you. Now, tell us what happened, starting with why you're here."

"I came here looking for Miss Mallone." Ness indicated Hopeful, who still sat beside me. "She got left behind yesterday in Independence. So did these young'uns. I spent all night searching for them back in town. Finally headed back up the trail this way and found them just now. Only when I did, that gentleman there thought I had other ideas." Ness sneered the word *gentleman* with elegant disdain. "Tried to shoot me 'cause I wouldn't agree with him as to whether or not I was a thief."

Sanderson snorted. "He'll say anything to save his hide."

Hauer said, "Let's hear your version."

Sanderson straightened up. "Happened the way you'd expect. I was making my rounds when I found this boy sneaking up on the camp, quiet as an Injun. I could see he was up to no good, so I stopped him. He tried feeding me one lie after another. Then he tried to take my gun away from me, and we tussled some. Next thing I knowed, he'd tried to shoot me with my own gun. I'm lucky you came up when you did, or there's no telling what might've happened."

"That's a lie!" I burst out, jumping to my feet. "I

saw the whole thing. Ness didn't take his gun away until after he'd fired it, trying to kill Ness."

Hauer beckoned to me. "About time we heard your side of things. You know this man Ness long?"

"Well, not real long," I admitted. "Just for the few days we been traveling with his wagon train. I mean the one his pa is the wagon master of."

"How come you Daltons and your friend Hopeful got left behind in Independence?"

Hopeful stood too, blanket pulled tight around her like a shawl. "My stepmother and I had a... a misunderstanding."

Hauer tipped his head to one side and studied her a long moment. "Over him?" he asked, nodding at Ness.

"In part, yes."

"But you weren't running off with him?"

"No. Ness had no notion I was... left behind, I don't think."

"Not until we made camp," Ness agreed.

Hauer stared at the ground, considering. Finally, he announced, "Sanderson, you're trigger-happy. I've suspected as much for a long time. I'm removing you from guard duty."

Sanderson growled, "You can't do that!"

"I can. You know that. I'm the wagon master." Hauer held out a hand. "I want your gun."

"You have it," Sanderson ground out between

clenched teeth.

"I mean your pistol."

"You're kidding."

"Just until we've got these youngsters safely back with their own wagon train. I don't want any more surprises." Hauer advanced until he stood almost toe-to-toe with Sanderson.

Sanderson shrugged off the two men holding his arms, bent down, and untied the leather thong that held his holster to his thigh like he was a fancy gunslinger in a dime novel. Then he unbuckled his gun belt and dropped the whole thing, pistol and all. He stalked away from the ring of wagons, into the morning mist.

Hauer heaved a regretful sigh. He picked up the gun belt and gave it to one of the men who'd brought Sanderson over to the impromptu trial. He tossed Sanderson's shotgun to the other man and told them both, "Keep an eye on him."

When the others had left, Hauer and Ness joined Hopeful and me. Hauer stopped beside the fire and studied us while Ness circled around to stand beside Hopeful.

Hauer took off his hat. "Are you hurt, any of you?" he asked. In the light of the fire, his swept-back hair shone. It was almost as dark as Hopeful and Ness's, but glossier.

"Not me," I said. Ness and Hopeful shook their

heads.

"Thank the good Lord," Hauer sighed.

"What happens to him?" Ness asked, jerking his thumb in the direction Sanderson had gone.

"Not much, I'm afraid."

"Can't we get a lawman from town to throw him in jail?"

"Don't think so. Sanderson was on guard duty. He found a stranger sneaking around camp and stopped him. He threatened you, but he didn't shoot you. Nobody got hurt."

Ness said, "And he's a white man, so that's where it ends, don't it."

"Some might see it that way. I'm sure this isn't the first time you've run up against his kind."

"Seems like the world's full of his kind."

"I know."

"You know." Ness made a noise that sounded almost like a laugh.

Hauer gave him a stern look. "I know because it's not my first time either. Oh, sure, I know my skin looks white enough. You see me and think, *There's a man who's got no idea what it is to be hated for what you are, not who you are, not what you've done or left undone. To be called names you didn't earn. Don't deserve.* But I do."

While Hauer spoke, Jacob came and stood beside me, quiet and solid.

Hauer continued, "What you don't know is, my ma was Cherokee. My pa was white. That meant I spent a lot of years getting told I didn't belong one place or another. I got blamed for plenty of things I didn't do. If a pie went missing or a garden got trampled or chickens disappeared, it was easy to blame the half-breed kid, not your own carelessness or your own children.

"Sure, it's not the same. These days, most folks can't tell by looking at me that I'm not just another white man. You couldn't yourself. But it's something like, anyhow. So, yes, I do know, at least a little."

Hopeful said softly, "I think you do."

Ness said, "You still won't do anything about that man trying to kill me."

"I'm taking him off guard duty for the rest of the trail. And I'll keep his guns until I see you safe back with your own wagon train. That's the most I can do."

"You could kick him out of your train," I offered. That sounded more like a punishment than taking him off guard duty and keeping his guns.

"I could." Hauer took me seriously. "But then what? He'd join another train. Maybe come after you and make more trouble 'cause he's sore. If I let him stay with us, I can keep an eye on him. Make sure he doesn't follow when you leave. That is, if you want to leave. You're welcome to stay on with us until you get where you're going, wherever that is."

"Junction City," Jacob said.

"We'll pass through there."

Ness shifted. "The Dalton kids can stay. As for us... I'll leave that up to Miss Mallone. Where she goes, I'll go."

Hopeful squeezed his hand. "I know. Mr. Hauer, do you think we could catch up with my folks? I'd like to tell my daddy goodbye."

"Expect we could if we hustled. I'll let folks know I want to make some good miles today. Should find your wagons by nightfall, at least." Hauer put his hat back on his head and left.

Jacob said, "Better get that breakfast going. And let's remember to make extra for lunch again. No apples to be had until we find the other train again." He sauntered off before I could do more than sputter in reply. Behind me, Laura laughed, then Lillie and Martha joined in, and I couldn't help but laugh too.

Something had changed in Jacob. I wasn't sure what, yet, but as long as he kept speaking to me, I was happy.

I was also happy we'd be stopping by the other wagon train so Hopeful could say her goodbyes. I wanted to see Mrs. Mallone one last time too. I told myself it was so I could thank her for what little she'd taught me about healing people, and so I could fix her beauty in my mind for all time.

But I think my real reason was that I still couldn't reconcile her behavior to Hopeful with her loveliness and her talent for healing. I couldn't forget the way she had slapped Hopeful, insulted her, shaken her. But I hadn't lost my admiration for her, either. And that contradiction bothered me more than I could admit to myself right then. I can see it and understand it now that I've had years to study on it, and now that I know everything that happened next. But there, in the middle of it all, I was simply muddled and hoping that seeing her would clear things up somehow.

CHAPTER SEVENTEEN

It was mid-afternoon when we came upon the Mallones' wagon train circled not far from the road. We rolled around a low hill, and there they were, stopped and silent. I didn't see or hear any children running about, and what people we did see stood in small groups. I found the quiet eerie. Even that Sunday we'd spent with them, camped a whole day for rest, there had been chatter, singing, movement.

Hauer had put us at the front that morning so we'd recognize Hopeful's wagon train when we met it. Driving in the lead instead of dragging at the tail end was a whole new way to travel. Almost as though it was just our two wagons and Hauer up ahead, not a whole passel of people.

When we came upon the stopped wagons, Hauer rode his pony over by Jacob and pointed at the camp. Jacob must have said yes, that was them, because Hauer called us to a halt on the trail. We waited while Hauer rode across the grass to the other train. I saw Wallace stride out to meet him. Hauer slid off his mount, and the two wagon masters had a discussion. I wished I could hear them. Why was the camp so quiet? Something must be wrong.

Behind us, people talked in hushed voices, like they were awed by the silence of the others.

Ness interrupted my musings by joining me on the opposite side of the road from the circle. "Levi, set your brake and climb down a minute."

I did as he asked, and he led me over to Jacob. Ness said, "I got a favor to beg of you two. Wallace turned me out. I can't go back in there, and—"

I interrupted him. I couldn't help it, bad manners or no. "He turned you out? Why?"

Ness shrugged. "I spoke my mind and he didn't care for it. I wouldn't mind so much, except for Hopeful. She'll go back there again. Even if it's just to say goodbye. And I can't watch out for her when she does."

"Watch out for her?" Jacob asked.

"Seeing as how her stepmother made Wallace leave her behind, I don't think she'll take kindly to Hopeful coming back, even for goodbyes."

"You know that for sure?" I asked. "That it wasn't Wallace's idea?"

"I didn't hear her tell him to leave Hopeful there,

if that's what you mean. But I know that's how it happened, just the same."

Jacob agreed, "We'll try to stick close to Hopeful. But we need a reason to go with her."

Ness nodded at me. "He's got reason enough."

Jacob raised his eyebrows. "How's that?"

I took a deep breath. "I asked her to teach me how to... to heal sick folks. I could say I wanted to thank her. Mrs. Mallone, I mean. For what little she taught me." I looked down. "I hoped I might do that anyhow."

"Right." Jacob shrugged. "If Levi is willing, he can go with Hopeful and I'll trail after him when I can."

"Thank you." Ness jumped on his big bay and rode on up around a bend and out of sight before we could change our minds. Or before Wallace spotted him, maybe.

Jacob eyed me. "Asked her to teach you how to heal folks?"

I frowned, defying what I took to be his disbelief that I could ever learn medicine or be of important use. "I did. I'm tired of people dying with nothing I can do to help." I stood straighter, hoping he'd see me as almost grown and able to do something that important.

"Ahhhh," was all he said. Then he gestured at something behind me. "Better get moving."

I spotted Hopeful striding off toward Hauer and

Wallace. Though I hurried off to catch up. I was still a few steps behind Hopeful when she neared the two wagon masters.

Hauer said, "I'm sorry, Miss Mallone."

"Sorry?" She stopped, maybe five feet away from them. "Sorry why?"

"Mr. Wallace here says there's sickness in this train. It's best you not go in there. Same for the little ones." His eyes flicked over to me, then back to Hopeful.

"Sickness? Who's sick?" Hopeful faced Wallace. "Who's sick?" she asked again.

"I'm hate to have to tell you this—" he began.

"Dear Jesus, no!" Hopeful cried out wildly. "Not gone, don't let him be gone. Not with me away!" She whirled and started for the wagons.

Wallace grabbed her by both arms. "We don't know if it's catching. He was fine yesterday, but this afternoon... he didn't wake."

Hopeful wrenched herself away from him. She rubbed her arms where he'd grabbed her. "I'd have been here," she said coldly. "If you hadn't left me in Independence, I'd have been here. I'd have stopped this."

"I tell you, your pa's sick." He stepped between her and the wagons. "I'm sorry about the other day. If I'd known this would happen, I wouldn't have persuaded you to stay behind."

"Persuaded?" Hopeful hugged her arms around herself. "*Persuaded* is the wrong word here, Wallace. Altogether the wrong word. I know it, you know it, your son knows it—even Levi here knows it. What has she promised you? What has she given you already?"

Wallace's eyebrows drew together and his eyes widened. He appeared about to vent a whole lot of fury on the person before him.

I opened my mouth to tell her to stop slandering her stepmother that way. That would only ruin her chances of seeing her father. But I stopped because of who I saw gliding over the uneven ground toward us, her gray dress soft and silent as a starless night.

"Hopeful!" Mrs. Mallone called, her voice a mix of relief and weariness. "Hopeful, you've come back to us. Thank the Lord. And Levi! Why, you'll be such a help. I'm so glad you found us again." She smiled straight at me, her face tired but still lovely.

Wallace's angry glare faded into confusion. Mrs. Mallone ignored him completely when she reached us. She put her arms around Hopeful, stroking her back and saying soft nothings to comfort her.

Hopeful stood stiff and straight, barely allowing her stepmother to embrace her.

Mrs. Mallone turned to Hauer, one arm around Hopeful's shoulders to keep her close. "I don't believe I know you, but I must thank you for bringing my daughter safely back to us." She smiled at Hauer, beautiful and serene, though her eyes held a world of tiredness.

Hopeful muttered, "Stepdaughter," but no one paid her any heed.

Hauer said, "Happy I could help her."

"Hey!" yelled a man from behind us. "How come we've stopped! What's the idea?" Sanderson jumped down from his wagon, as peeved as if he were the wagon master instead of Hauer. He marched right over, glaring at Hauer, but slowed when he saw Mrs. Mallone. I expected him to sneer and insult her the way he had Hopeful. But he shocked me. "Well, good afternoon to you." He tipped his hat as he looked her up and down boldly like she was a bolt of calico at a dry goods store.

I wanted to punch him. I wanted to jab his eyes out for looking at her that way. Only fourteen and still innocent of much of the world's sinful side, I still knew he had no business eyeing her all hungry-like.

"I'm afraid it's not a good afternoon here. You see, my husband...." Tears filled her eyes.

"Oh." Sanderson took a step back. "I apologize. If there's anything I can do to help, ma'am, just ask for Sanderson. I do apologize."

"No matter. But thank you anyhow."

"Any time." Sanderson swept off his hat, gaze still fastened on her. "Any time at all." He grinned at her, probably thinking he looked like a charming gentleman. But he put me in mind of a cat who'd spotted a mouse.

Mrs. Mallone smiled sadly at Wallace, "I am sorry about the misunderstanding about my girl. Let's all forget it, shall we?"

Wallace opened his mouth, then closed it and shrugged.

"Come along, Hopeful. You too, Levi. I have plenty to keep you both busy." Mrs. Mallone nodded to Sanderson and Hauer. "Nice to have met you, gentlemen."

"The pleasure is all mine," Sanderson almost purred.

Hauer touched his hat. To me, he said, "I'll camp us a ways up the road, out of earshot so we won't disturb the sick. Follow the road and you'll find us."

"Yes, sir. Unless..." I made myself look Wallace in the eye, trying not to show that he scared me almost beyond speaking. "Unless we could join back up with you?"

Wallace frowned. "We'll stay camped here until... while the sickness lasts. You want to get to Junction City and your uncle quick, I thought."

"I do. I mean, we do. But..." I dropped my eyes, not able to stand his scrutiny any longer.

Hauer said, "We'll talk that out tomorrow. Get along now, kid. Don't keep the lady waiting. I'll tell your family where you are."

"Yes, sir." I followed Mrs. Mallone and Hopeful. I didn't know how I'd be able to protect Hopeful without Jacob. Though half of my mind tried to puzzle that out, the other half exulted over the fact that Mrs. Mallone had said I could help her. Help her nurse her ailing husband and maybe anyone else who might fall ill, too. It was my chance to learn some real doctoring at last.

The Mallone wagon sat clear on the other side of the circle, parked as far from the road as could be. It was outside the wagon circle, set back some for more privacy and quiet. Or to keep the disease from spreading.

The whole train held its breath so as not to disturb the ailing preacher. I wouldn't let myself use the word "dying" regarding him. Not yet. No one else had said it, so I would not think that word unless... but I didn't let myself think about that either. No more graves and funerals and mourning, not for me. I refused to think of it. Mrs. Mallone would save her husband, and I would help her.

The canvas cover over the Mallone wagon was puckered shut with its drawstring. When we reached it, Mrs. Mallone picked up a bucket and held it out. "Fetch me some water, Levi."

I took the bucket's rope handle. "Which way to the river?"

"Yonder." She indicated a line of slender trees.

"Yes, ma'am." I stepped away, then remembered my promise to Ness. Jacob had not yet joined us, so it was up to me to stay with Hopeful. I stopped. "Hopeful? Could you come along?"

She paused, one foot on the steps and one on the ground. "What for?" she asked, her voice flat.

"It's just, Ness told me not to wander around alone. Some people don't like... me. Being here."

Mrs. Mallone stood at the top of the stairs, untying the cord that held the cover tight. "Get a move on. I need that water." She looked stern, even disappointed.

I groped desperately for something that would convince them both. "Our first day with you, this man, he scared me. He was huge. And angry. And I don't want to meet up with him alone again."

"Samson, I suppose." Mrs. Mallone sighed. "Very well."

Hopeful asked, "Wait while I look in on my daddy first?"

"Sure," I agreed.

Mrs. Mallone finished loosening the cover's opening and ducked inside the dark wagon. Hopeful followed her, and I stood at the foot of the steps, watching the two women kneel beside the reverend's still body. Hopeful laid her hand on her father's chest and bent down to kiss his cheek. Then she backed out and down the steps. "Let's go." She didn't even glance at me. Off we went to the river, empty bucket knocking against my legs, we walked so fast.

As soon as we reached the water, Hopeful looked carefully around us, then asked, "What did Ness say to you and Jacob back at your wagons?" She kept her voice low, like she was afraid her stepmother had followed us there.

"That he can't come back here. Wallace turned him out."

"That all?"

"He asked us to stay near you. Watch over you."

"Oh, that Ness." She squeezed my hand once. "Thank you, Levi."

CHAPTER EIGHTEEN

When we got back from the river, dusk had settled over the camp. Mrs. Mallone sat on the top step, talking with three women. Two of them held plates of food. A third plate rested on Mrs. Mallone's knees, its food looking untouched.

One of the women held out a plate to Hopeful, who took it with a small smile. The other woman who held food glared at me, but said nothing.

"Where do you want this, ma'am?" I asked Mrs. Mallone, holding forth the water bucket.

"Bring it up inside. And get something to eat." She gestured at the plate of food the third woman held.

"But I made this for the Reverend Eli," protested the woman.

Mrs. Mallone shook her head. "He can't eat a thing. Might as well give it to the boy. And thank you again for your kindness."

"What's this boy doing back here?" The woman still didn't offer me the food. "Thought we were rid of those hangers-on."

"He's come to help me. I been teaching him some about healing. If more folks take sick, I'll need all the help I can come by."

The woman still hesitated. Mrs. Mallone took the plate off her own lap and held it down to me. "Eat, child. Then bring that water up to me inside."

I took the tin plate. It contained one big sweet potato, skin charred black from baking it in ashes, plus a hoecake and a mess of stewed greens. No fork or spoon. "Thank you, ma'am." I picked up the hoecake.

The three women left, the third clutching her plate of food like she thought I'd snatch it from her. Mrs. Mallone climbed back inside.

Once I'd finished eating, I picked up the bucket and lugged it up the steps. Inside, the Reverend Eli lay covered with a woolen blanket. Mrs. Mallone crouched at his head, her box of medicines open beside her. Hopeful sat on a crate between me and her stepmother, her skirt bunched up around her feet. She held her father's hand and stroked its back from wrist to finger tips, over and over.

Humming softly, Mrs. Mallone checked over her supply of herbs and remedies. She would hold one up to the light and shake it, then frown and put it back and take out another. When she saw me, she picked up a tin cup. "Fill this halfway with water," she instructed, giving it to Hopeful, who passed it to me.

I set the bucket down on the top step and dipped the cup in it. I poured some out again until I judged it to be half full, then carefully handed it back.

Mrs. Mallone took out a glass bottle filled almost to the brim with a milky liquid. "Watch close, now," she told me. "This is laudanum. Just a bit brings peaceful sleep. But a little too much, and a body will never wake again. Got to measure it by drops."

She put both bottle and cup down and reached up for a lantern hanging from one of the wooden hoops that held the canvas wagon cover up. "I need more light," she told me. "Light this at a fire. I've got no matches."

I hopped down and hustled over to the circle of wagons. I ignored all the people, though I knew they were staring at me. Using a wisp of straw, I lit the lantern from the nearest fire.

Jacob found me on my way back. "Everything all right?" he asked.

"The Reverend Eli is bad off," I said. "Won't wake."

"You left Hopeful?"

I stopped. "I did. I—I made her go to the river

with me, but just now... I didn't think."

"Better hurry back, then." Jacob glanced around us. "I can't stay. I need to get the horses settled. And everyone else, too. I'll be back when I can."

"All right."

"Don't leave her again. Remember that. You promised Ness."

"I'll remember." Scurrying back to the wagon, I clambered up the front wheel and gave the lantern to Mrs. Mallone over the wagon seat. By its light, I could see Hopeful still holding her father's hand.

"We need strong light to see by," Mrs. Mallone explained. "Got to be careful with laudanum. You watch close now. I need you to know how. I've had no sleep for nearly two days, and if I have to sleep and he gets restless again, you'll need to give him another dose, you hear?"

"I hear." I watched closely as she tipped the bottle above the cup. One drop, two drops, more and more until I'd counted fifteen of them.

"It's fifteen drops in half a cup of water," Mrs. Mallone told me. "You got that?"

I repeated, "Fifteen drops in half a cup of water."

"Good." She stoppered up the bottle and placed it beside her medicine chest. Then she leaned down, lifted the Reverend Eli's head, and placed the cup to his lips. "Drink, husband. Drink and rest."

The Reverend Eli's eyes barely fluttered open. It

seemed to me he swallowed the mixture without knowing it. When she laid his head on the pillow again, his face slackened with unconsciousness.

"Tell me again, Levi. How many drops and how much water?"

"Fifteen drops and half a cup," I replied, proud of my new knowledge.

"Only if he gets restless, you hear?" She yawned. "I got to sleep or I'll drop right here." She looked over at Hopeful. "I've a mind to spread your tent and sleep there."

Hopeful stood. "I'll help you." She picked up her rolled-up tent canvas.

"No, no, I'll manage. You stay with your papa. I know he's missed you." Mrs. Mallone took up the canvas roll, sidled past her daughter, and left through the back of the wagon. Outside, she said, "Why thank you, Wallace. I could use some help with this tent."

Wallace replied too low for me to hear. I paid no heed, for my attention was focused on the box beside me, gleaming in all its polished glory. Containing all those secrets and remedies, and there I sat, learning about them. Left in charge of dosing a patient. I felt like a man grown.

From outside, Mrs. Mallone called to me loud and clear, "Levi, you remembering how many drops and how much water?"

"Fifteen drops and half a cup," I answered.

"Good boy." She heaved the water bucket up to the seat behind me.

Near her stood Wallace, beside the tent he'd helped her set up. Mrs. Mallone put her hand on his arm. "Thank you for the help, Wallace. This will do nicely. I'm so glad of the chance to rest, I could have fallen asleep with nothing over my head at all."

"Anything I can do to help, you let me know." He rested his hand over hers for a moment.

"Thank you. I will, I promise you." She turned to me, her hand still on his arm, tucked under his. "When you get sleepy, Levi, you come and wake me. All I need is an hour or two. You wake me when you can't keep watch anymore." Then she ducked down into the tent.

Wallace faced me a moment, though I couldn't read his expression in the deepening twilight. He strode away without speaking.

CHAPTER NINETEEN

I jolted back to wakefulness for the third time. Rubbed my eyes. Tried to figure out why I woke, and felt ashamed for having drifted off again.

Something jostled my left foot. That's what had brought me out of my dozing, I realized. I turned the lamp up and saw that the Reverend Eli's eyes had opened. He twitched his fingers up near my foot.

I shook my head until I was awake enough to remember Mrs. Mallone's instructions. She'd said if the Reverend Eli got restless, then he needed more medicine.

I fumbled around for the tin cup and dipped it in the water bucket. Half full, I recalled. Then I found the little glass bottle of laudanum she'd left out for me. I held the tin cup up near the lantern and tipped the bottle above it while, one by one, fifteen drops plopped into the water.

Once I had the bottle safely stoppered up again, I focused on my patient. My very first patient. "Here, this will help." I leaned down, doing my best to be gentle and careful.

The Reverend Eli turned his head away, then back to me again. He tried to speak, but no words left his moving lips. I thought maybe he was praying. I dared to put my hand under his head so I could lift it and make it easier for him to drink his medicine without spilling. I raised his head up some and put the cup to his lips. He stared up at me, his eyes pleading for... something. I didn't know what. Water, maybe. I remembered Aunt Phoebe and Uncle Drew asking for water over and over.

"Go on," I encouraged him softly. "Drink it up, if you're thirsty. I can get more water if you finish it. I have a whole bucket here."

He swallowed some, made a face, and tried to push the cup away. "No," he mumbled around the cup I held pressed against his lips. "No more."

"I'm supposed to give you all of it," I insisted, and tilted the cup higher, pouring it into his mouth. He swallowed reflexively, but much of it dribbled down his chin.

Well, I'd done my best. He'd drunk most of it, anyhow. And it seemed to help, for he soon drifted off again, his breathing even and his limbs slack once more.

I set the cup beside the laudanum bottle and settled on top of the chest where I'd perched before, leaning against the back of the wagon seat. I glanced over at Hopeful, who lay curled up on a pile of quilts. She'd never stirred the whole time I soothed her father. Watching her sleep made me sleepy too, but I was determined to give Mrs. Mallone as much rest as I could. To prove I could keep watch over an ailing person as well as any adult. After all, if I meant to be a doctor one day, I'd have to learn to sit up all night with the sick.

I turned the lamp down a bit to save oil the way Aunt Phoebe had taught me and tried doing sums in my head again to keep awake. It worked for a while, though my dozing off from time to time showed it wasn't entirely effective.

The next time I woke up, I could have sworn something had brushed against my arm. A touch so light I almost hadn't noticed it. Something rustled across the grass outside. Had an animal tried to get in? Or a person? I turned up the lantern and looked about me. The laudanum bottle seemed farther from the medicine chest than I remembered, but I wasn't certain. Nothing else looked disturbed. The Reverend Eli slept on. I decided I must have imagined it.

Then a voice beside me almost made me jump

clear out of the wagon. "You're tired, Levi," said Mrs. Mallone kindly. "You've earned some rest. I've slept plenty."

I realized arguing would be silly, since she'd undoubtedly seen me nodding off. That must have been her that I heard, rustling the grass as she left the tent. "Yes, ma'am." I scrambled down.

"Here, have a drink of water before you sleep." She held out a tin cup. "You must be thirsty, staying awake so long."

"Thank you." I swallowed half the water in one gulp and grimaced. "I think maybe we need to wash that cup. Tastes strange," I told her, tossing the rest of the water onto the grass.

"Oh! I'm sorry. I'll do that." She took the cup back from me with an odd half smile and shooed me toward the tent. "Best get some rest while you can. Sun'll be up soon."

I crawled into Hopeful's tent, my head and hands heavy. Sleep, that's all I needed. Sleep.

But a thought nibbled at my brain. I'd promised someone something.

I'd promised Ness. That I wouldn't leave Hopeful. And now, here I was, falling asleep in her tent while she lay in the wagon alone. But she wasn't alone. Her stepmother and father were there. My muddled thoughts chased each other around and around. What did alone mean, anyway? And Jacob had said he'd follow me. Where was Jacob?

I tossed my head. My thoughts buzzed around, and I found I couldn't draw a deep breath. But I felt a desperate urge to get out of that tent and go find Jacob right then, middle of the night or not.

I crawled my way out of the tent, slowly, feeble as a baby. Jacob. I needed to ask him something. Or tell him something? Wobbling and swaying, I made my way around the wagon, staggering off toward the road.

But I never made it to the road. I didn't make it more than thirty feet before a wave of illness crashed into me, tumbling me to the ground. My stomach lurched. The water I'd just drunk, plus the remains of that plateful of food, all landed in the grass. My insides heaved again and again. Gradually, my mind cleared some. And a terrible fear seized me.

What if I had the fever?

I pushed myself up to my feet and stumbled my way back, avoiding the place where I'd been sick. Mrs. Mallone had medicine. Mrs. Mallone would help me. I found the stairs and fell against them, trying to crawl up inside of the wagon.

It looked lighter inside than I remembered, as though the lamp was turned up high. I would have tried to guess why, if I'd had any space left in my brain for anything but the fear that I'd gotten the fever and the hope that Mrs. Mallone could cure me.

I sprawled out on those steps, working hard just to breathe. I could barely see inside the wagon bed, and I opened my mouth to call out for help. But what I saw stopped me, for it confused me and drove my earlier thoughts clean out of my mind.

Mrs. Mallone knelt beside her husband, beneath the bright lantern. Her beautiful medicine box stood open, and I could see the glass bottles glittering inside. She removed one bottle at the front, the middle one, and thrust her fingers down inside the box in the place where it had been. I heard a little *click*. The secret drawer she'd told me of slid open just enough to show it had unlocked. Mrs. Mallone put the bottle back, then gently pulled the drawer until it opened to reveal two slender vials.

Mrs. Mallone picked up the vial on the left. It was half-filled with a grayish liquid. It looked somewhat like laudanum, but thicker. She held it up to the lantern light, swirling the contents. Then she kissed the glass and whispered words my ears half-caught. They sounded like *Hello, hebona, old friend*. After uncorking the vial, she picked up a tin cup and poured the tiniest amount of the thick gray substance into the cup, maybe only a drop or two.

Quickly, she recorked the vial and laid it back in the secret drawer. With a nod of satisfaction, she set the cup down, closed drawer and lid both, then knelt beside her husband.

Her hands looked gentle as she raised his head with one and held the cup in the other, ready for him to drink. They looked gentle, but I soon saw they were not.

The Reverend Eli's eyes opened wide. "No!" He groaned the word. Not even my aunt and uncle's dying breaths had sounded as piteous. "No. You leave us be." He struggled feebly, trying to push Mrs. Mallone's hands away.

Her hands clutched him like claws, one pinching at his shoulder to hold him in place, the other pushing the cup against his lips. "Hush, now," Mrs. Mallone muttered. "Take your medicine."

The Reverend Eli tried to turn away from the cup. "I won't. I saw it. I won't drink it."

"If you don't," his wife hissed, "I'll give it to her. To the girl. Your girl."

The Reverend Eli stopped struggling. "Leave her be," he repeated. Then he allowed her to tip the cup up, pouring its contents into his mouth. I thought he would spit the concoction out, but he rolled his face toward Hopeful, who lay slumped near me, her eyes closed, her breathing shallow. He swallowed with a grimace.

Mrs. Mallone laughed as she dropped his head, letting it thud back onto his thin pillow. She scooted back to her medicine box and opened it again. I watched, mesmerized, as she repeated her actions, measuring out another tiny dose into a little water and swirling it together. Then she edged forward on her knees again, aiming for Hopeful this time.

I must have whimpered in fright. With a gasp, she lifted her face and looked straight at me. "Who's there?" she cried, her voice high and thin. "Who's there?"

I bolted. Before she could make her way to one end of the wagon or the other to chase me, I'd ducked down inside the tent where I was meant to be asleep. Why, I didn't know, but I could see she wanted me asleep. I flopped down, shut my eyes, and willed my limbs to go limp.

Down the stairs she came, every footstep louder than the last. The night air rushed in when she opened the tent flap. I kept my eyes closed and made my breathing as even as I could. She stood there a long time, or so it felt. Finally, she let the tent flap fall again. I heard it swish down against the grass, but still I kept my eyes closed. Aunt Phoebe used to come check on us when we'd been whispering and giggling in the dark. She would pretend to leave, but then she'd stand there all quiet until we'd think she was gone. We'd start whispering again, and she'd catch us as guilty as could be. I kept on pretending, just in case.

Then I heard Wallace's say, "Everything all right, Lucretia?" His murmured words sounded so close I knew I could have touched him if not for the tent canvas between us.

"Oh, yes," Mrs. Mallone answered. "Just settling Levi in the tent and taking my turn watching." She lowered her voice even more than his and added, "I fear for my girl. She's not looking well."

"Fever?"

"We'll know soon enough."

"Since you're awake, can you spare a moment?"

"For you? Always." Her voice sounded sweet as could be now, nothing like the frightful hiss it had been back in the wagon.

"Would you look in on Sarah and her young'uns? Two of them been coughing."

Mrs. Mallone paused. "Oh. Yes, of course. Lend me your arm and lead me to them, will you? I don't see well in the dark."

When I heard their footsteps rustling away, I risked opening my eyes. The tent flap was shut. I scooted over to it as softly as I could and opened it a little, figuring if they saw, I could say their talking had wakened me. But they had almost reached the circled wagons, the lantern Mrs. Mallone held sailing smoothly along and lighting her gray skirts so they looked like a ghostly figure moving alone.

I shivered as I crawled out and hurried to the wagon. "Hopeful?" I whispered as I climbed up the steps, still unsteady and weak, but too desperate to mind. "Hopeful?" If she didn't have a fever yet, I feared she'd soon get it from staying near her father. I needed to get her away.

She didn't answer, so I jostled her shoulder. "Hopeful?" It was too dark inside for me to see much, and Mrs. Mallone had taken the only lantern with her. I had no way to find the cup she'd dosed the Reverend Eli with. I wished I could see it so I'd know if she'd made Hopeful drink it, or if my noise had interrupted her before she could.

Hopeful stirred. "Who's there?" she asked, her words slow, but not slurred.

"It's me, Levi. Are you feverish? Can you walk?"

"Walk? It's night. Walk where?"

"Anywhere that's not here." I instinctively wanted to get her away before Mrs. Mallone returned. And get myself away too. Somehow, though I'd depended on her to cure me of my ailment, I worried she would not do the same for Hopeful. And I couldn't keep close by Hopeful if I took sick. I needed to get her back to Jacob and Ness. They'd know what to do.

"Why?"

"Ness wants to see you," I lied.

"All right." She sat up and scooted toward me, more slowly than I'd like, but not weak and shaky the way I still was. Hopeful wrapped her blanket around herself and followed me. "Where is he?" she asked, not whispering.

"Shhhhhh! He's... back at the other wagon train. With Jacob." Which was possible, I reasoned. At any rate, it was a safer place than here, where people came down with fevers and who knows what else.

Together, we stumbled through the darkness, back to the road and then on down it until we could make out the huddled white canvas tops of the other wagon train. I hadn't thought this far. Who was on guard? It wouldn't be that horrid Sanderson, at least, but what if it was someone equally unfriendly? Would they remember me, that I'd been with them earlier that day? Would they go get Jacob to identify me?

And when Hopeful found out I'd lied about Ness wanting to see her, would she go straight back to her father and all the contagion and death surrounding anyone with a fever?

I had no answers for my own questions. When a man's voice challenged me out of the darkness with, "Who's there?" I couldn't even answer him.

I tried to say, "It's us, Levi Dalton and Hopeful." But instead, I moaned, "Where's Jacob?" as the land tilted under my feet and I seemed to slide to the ground more than fall.

CHAPTER TWENTY

My first question when I awoke was the same as my last: "Where's Jacob?"

"He'll be right back. Don't fret, now." That was Hopeful's voice, clear and sure of itself the same as when I'd first met her.

I tried to blink away the weak sunshine coming through the openings at either end of the wagon. I should tell her what I'd seen her stepmother doing, how she'd forced the Reverend Eli to drink medicine from her secret drawer. Or maybe I ought to yell for Jacob to find Ness and stop Mrs. Mallone from pouring that *hebona* stuff down the throats of people she should be helping.

I found myself convinced that it was not the remedy for bringing folks back to health she'd spoken of a few days earlier. Not with the way she'd had to force the Reverend Eli to take it. But maybe what she'd given him had been something to ease his final time. Dying of fever wasn't something I'd wish anyone to go through. I'd seen it too close-up.

That brought back the idea that I might be dying of fever. It I was, Hopeful shouldn't be anywhere near me. "Get away," I croaked, my throat raw.

"Shhh. Jacob'll be here in a minute, and your sisters too." She'd perched on a throne of pillows all stacked up.

"No!" I pushed myself up on my elbows and looked around wildly, assuring myself no one else was there. "No, they can't! They'll catch it!"

"Catch what?" Hopeful squinted at me. "Did you hit your head when you fell? That why you slept this long?" She reached out and felt my head all over before I could stop her. "Don't feel any lumps. Can you see straight?"

"Catch the fever, that's what!" I jerked away from her.

Hopeful laughed, light and sweet as April rain. "You've got no fever, Levi."

"I do! I caught it from your pa! It came on all of a sudden, just like Uncle Drew and Aunt Phoebe." I almost sobbed those two names, thinking about how soon I'd be seeing them again.

"You've had no fever, Levi." Hopeful's tone turned stern so fast, it stopped my tears.

"I have too. I couldn't hardly stand, and I... I...

got sick of a sudden."

"You got sick, yes, but not from fever. Sick from something she gave you." She had lost all cheer and sympathy.

"Something she gave me?" I remembered, fuzzily, thinking the water had tasted funny. Hadn't I had a suspicion about it? That it had something in it that would make me sleep? I couldn't rightly remember.

"She tried it on me too. But I poured most of it down my dress and only pretended it made me sleep. Levi, you must tell me—what did you see last night in that wagon?"

I shook my head, annoyed. "I didn't see anything. I gave your pa laudanum the way she said to. And then… I felt sick."

"And then you tried to get back in. I know you saw something. I was awake, but I couldn't turn my head to watch her, not without letting her know I wasn't drugged. You're my only witness, Levi. You've got to tell the truth. Tell me, and then we'll get help. From that Hauer man, maybe. Ness will know. But first, tell me what you saw."

I closed my eyes, my thoughts spinning so crazily I thought the wagon might whirl in a circle to match. "I didn't see anything."

Hopeful groaned. "Levi, you too?"

I kept my eyes tight closed and tried to remember what Mrs. Mallone had told me about the medicine in that drawer. *Things to cure, and things to destroy*, she'd said. I'd seen two vials there. She'd used one. Which was which? How could I know for sure if she'd been hurting her husband and not helping him? I'd sensed a deep wrongness in what I'd seen, but could I tell that to Hauer? To Wallace? Her giving a sick man medicine wasn't proof of anything, was it?

True, she'd threatened to give Hopeful the potion, as though it would harm her, but maybe that was because what healed a sick person could harm a healthy one. Maybe that's why the Reverend Eli had drunk it up after her threat.

Hopeful sighed. "Lord, have mercy. Young or old, rich or poor, she'll make fools of them all in the end. How'm I going to set you straight?"

"I'm not a fool."

"Maybe not. Maybe you're too innocent to see."

I waited for her to say more, but she didn't. Eventually, curiosity won out and I opened my eyes. "To see what?" I asked.

"To see she's using you the same way she uses everyone else. You're one more tool for her, like a spade or a plow in the hands of a farmer. She'll get what use she can out of you and then toss you aside."

I sat up, all thoughts of having a fever long gone. "Is that why you hate her?"

"Hate her? No. I don't hate her, Levi. I hate what

she does, that's all. To my daddy, to Wallace, and now to you."

"What's that?"

"Just what I've been saying. Used you. All of you. Used my daddy for his fine house and the respect folks pay him. Used me too, to fetch and carry for her, and clean and cook and anything else needs doing."

"And Wallace? And me?"

"Wallace, I don't rightly know. She likes that he's handsome and respected and got a place of his own already. Doesn't have to build a house. Doesn't have to claim land. She likes the idea of his house and his ranch, I know that. Likes hearing him talk about them. Says she wishes she had a real house waiting for her instead of whatever my daddy can scrape together at first, some shanty or dugout. She sure does want a real house, right away. And I guess she uses him to make herself feel pretty and important. He asks for her advice, brings her things, fusses over her. She likes it when folks fawn on her and give her gifts. Same reason she liked having you hanging about, at first."

"At first?"

"I don't know what she plans now. But she's got some plan, be sure of that. Some use she's keeping you around for."

"I did what she wanted, I kept watch. I gave your

pa his medicine."

"So you did." She looked worried. "You stay here. I'll be back in a minute or two," she promised before slipping out.

Jacob and Laura climbed in the wagon after Hopeful left. They found me still sitting on the mattress, a quilt over my knees, my chin resting on my fists. "I see you're awake," Laura said.

Jacob added, "About time."

I glared at him. "Do I have the fever?"

Laura gasped.

Jacob gave me Uncle Drew's canteen. "The fever? No, don't think so. Hopeful says you stayed up too late watching over the Reverend Eli, then drank out of the same cup you dosed him with and got a little laudanum in you. Made you sick. But you'll be fine once you get some food and water."

I stopped drinking from the canteen. "Hopeful said that?" I tried to think back. Had it been the same cup? Had it been an accident? "Where is she?" I asked.

"She went off to collect more firewood for breakfast. Said she needed to think. I figured she was safe enough here. I let her go."

"I've got to talk with her." I downed another couple swallows of water, tossed the canteen back to him, and kicked off the quilt. "I've got to find her right now." I clambered down to the ground and looked all around the camp. Where would she have gone to find firewood? The trees by the river.

Inside my mind, my words to Hopeful repeated over and over. *I gave your pa his medicine.* What if that was Mrs. Mallone's plan? What if she meant to give her husband something evil, such as that *hebona* stuff, when him dying would look like my fault? When everyone knew she'd left me in charge of dosing him with medicine. What if I'd let her use me exactly the way Hopeful said?

Ignoring Laura's insistence that I needed to eat something, I trotted away from the wagons.

CHAPTER TWENTY-ONE

I still have nightmares about that day, all these years later. About how hard I tried not to think about Mrs. Mallone and her medicine box. About the way I tried not to wonder what she might be doing with it right then. About how long it took me to find Hopeful perched in a tree near the river.

I peered up at her through the branches and said simply, "I saw her give your pa something from that secret drawer. Something in one of those two little vials."

"Was it red?"

"No. More grayish."

Hopeful didn't bother climbing down from the tree, she just dropped to the ground in front of me, light as a cat. "We got to go stop her."

"What is it?" I followed her as she marched off. "What's *hebona*, anyway?"

"Don't rightly know. But I saw inside that drawer once. One gray vial, and one red. She saved an old woman who lived next door. With the red medicine."

I stopped walking. "What if we're too late?" I remembered again what Mrs. Mallone had said. *Things to cure and things to destroy.* If the red had saved a woman....

Hopeful stared at me, eyes wide with fear. "Pray, Levi," she said. "Pray and run."

I didn't bother detouring around Wallace's wagon train, I barreled right across the wide space inside the circle. I raced past all the women making food and the men talking in small groups. I hoped that when I reached the wagon, I could climb right up the steps at its back like I had nothing to hide. If Mrs. Mallone didn't know what we suspected, what I'd seen, I could maybe stop anything else bad from happening until Hopeful got there. Maybe someone would see us running toward the wagon and follow, or call Wallace. Though I didn't know just whose side Wallace would be on. Maybe I should have gone back to the other wagon train, found Hauer or Jacob or Ness. But it was too late for that now.

When I arrived, Mrs. Mallone stood outside her wagon, packing something into a basket. I slowed down, but not soon enough to keep Mrs. Mallone from seeing what a hurry I'd been in.

"Whoa there, child." Her voice sounded bright, but not kind. "You'll get where you're going soon enough."

"Yes, Ma'am. How are you this morning?"

"Too early to tell yet." She smiled, so beautiful in her soft black dress it nearly broke my heart to think what she might be capable of.

"You need anything this morning? Water fetched, maybe?" I made myself keep right on walking toward her, same as if it was any other morning. As if I was still the boy who trusted her. As if I had no suspicion she planned on blaming me for her own misdeeds.

"No, I don't need a thing. I thought you might, though." She picked up the basket and held it out. "Been a while since we shared these with you. I picked them out of the barrel special for you this morning. I thought I'd have my girl bring you these, as a farewell present, but I've not seen her. Have you?"

"Yes." I stepped close enough to see her basket held apples. "I was just with her, over on the other side of the circle."

"Ah." Mrs. Mallone looked over my shoulder. "Why, here she comes now."

I turned and saw Hopeful. She held her head high, the picture of determination.

"Here," Mrs. Mallone held out the basket. "Take

them, please. There's plenty for your sisters and you, and your cousins too. Eat one on your way, and you can all have the rest with your breakfast." She kept right on smiling and talking. "Go ahead, they'll never know if you eat one on the way back. I picked those out special for you. Found all the best ones. I know you'll like them. We've got more than we'll ever eat. I'm glad we can share some with you."

I gazed at the apples. They were shiny, like she'd polished them on her apron. Why? But then... why not? I didn't want to make her suspicious by not doing as she asked. I picked up the top apple, brighter red than any apple I'd ever seen before, and shinier too. Almost unnaturally shiny. "Thank you, ma'am," I said.

Hopeful darted toward me. "Let me have that, Levi." She snatched it right out of my hand.

I stared at her, shocked.

"Hopeful! No!" Mrs. Mallone cried out. She tried to sound calm again. "Where are your manners?"

"I pray you'll pardon me." I couldn't tell if Hopeful said that to me or to her stepmother. Her mouth opened wide, teeth flashing white against the glossy red skin of that apple. She tore a great bite from it, a bite so big her mouth almost didn't close around it.

And then, without a sound, she crumpled to the ground.

I stood frozen with horror, unable to think or

move. I could only stare down at Hopeful. She lay on the grass, stiff and still, the apple she'd bitten into lying beside her empty hand.

Mrs. Mallone stepped backward. "Foolish girl," she murmured, her tone mocking. "Always such a foolish and headstrong girl." Then her eyes locked on mine. "What have you done?" she cried out, her voice rising with each word. "What have you done to my girl?"

I shook my head, wordless still.

Mrs. Mallone pointed a finger at me. "You killed her! Why did you kill her?" She looked over at the wagon circle. "Wallace!" she screamed. "Help me, Wallace!" She ran off, yelling for him as loud as she could. Her black skirts billowed behind her like a crow skimming the earth.

My legs gave out under me, and I sat down on the ground so suddenly my tailbone protested. The basket thumped down beside me, spilling apples everywhere. I scarcely noticed. I felt as if I'd choked on that poisoned apple. It had been meant for me. Mrs. Mallone had tried to poison me. Or had she? Had she expected Hopeful to take it from me, and that way she could blame me for this too? Or was that an accident?

Betrayal stung me through my numb shock. It twisted and burned inside me. Hopeful was dead. All my hopes, all my dreams had crumbled to ashes.

Hopeful had been right to fear her stepmother. And I'd failed Hopeful, not her stepmother. I'd been right here to take the blame, just the way Mrs. Mallone wanted.

Tears ran down my cheeks, hot with wrath. Hopeful, my aunt and uncle, my baby cousin, my own parents—I cried a flood of tears, trying to fill the aching hole they'd all left inside me.

But I hadn't sat there crying a whole minute, even, when someone dropped to their knees on the ground between me and Hopeful. Through my tears, I saw that it was Ness.

"No, Lord." With a sob, Ness bent over and kissed her forehead. "Not her. Not her. Never her. O Lord, why? Why'd you let this happen? Haven't you got enough angels already up there with you?"

I thought the tears in my eyes were playing tricks, for it seemed her eyelids fluttered. And then I knew it was no illusion, for her eyes flew wide open. She rolled onto her stomach and raised herself up on her arms enough to spit out that bite of apple. She spat again and again, coughing, gagging, clearing her mouth of all it had held.

Ness skittered backward, away from Hopeful, as if he'd been burnt. "What in the—"

"Water," Hopeful croaked. "Quick! Water." Her words sounded thick, as if her mouth was still filled with the apple.

Ness swooped Hopeful up in his arms. "I'll get you to water," he promised. He looked up, listening to something I couldn't hear yet. "She's coming back. Act dead."

Hopeful slumped in his arms, head rolling back and limbs going slack. I turned around and saw Mrs. Mallone clinging to Wallace and dragging him along. Behind them trailed a dozen or more people from the wagon train.

CHAPTER TWENTY-TWO

"He's killed her!" Mrs. Mallone shrieked. "Killed my girl!" She whirled to look at her wagon. "And if he killed her, what about my—" She gasped theatrically. "Oh, no! Not him too!" She let go of Wallace and flew across the grass to the wagon. When she ducked inside, she let out an eerie wail. No words, just noisy grief.

Wallace ran after her, though the other people stayed clustered around us. He reached the steps as Mrs. Mallone came back out. She climbed down two steps, then crumpled neatly into Wallace's arms. She hadn't fainted, however, and continued weeping as he lowered her to the ground. I noticed she held onto him in a way that ensured he had to keep his arms around her. What had Hopeful told me about her stepmother wanting to use Wallace? I could finally see what she'd meant.

Ness rose, still cradling Hopeful. He walked away from them all, moving woodenly, like a man would when dazed with grief. I got up too and followed him, leaving the basket of apples behind. I didn't know how many of them she'd poisoned, nor why Mrs. Mallone would have tried to kill me with them. I didn't care.

"Don't let him leave!" Mrs. Mallone cried out. "Stop them! Don't let that boy take my daughter!"

I looked back, scared. Ness kept on walking.

Wallace strode over to us. Only when he'd come within an arm's length did Ness stop.

"Best stay here." Wallace reached out a hand to Hopeful and Ness.

"Don't you touch her!" Ness warned him fiercely. "Nobody touches her!" He spoke loud enough for all to hear. "I loved Hopeful, you hear?" He shifted her body, hugging it even closer. "I loved her, and she loved me. We could've made each other happy, but no. No, you pushed us apart. Well, not again." He stared Wallace in the face. "You told me to leave, and that's what I'm doing." He stalked away. I followed him, stumbling as I tried to keep up.

Mrs. Mallone screamed, shrill and horrible. "Stop that white boy! He killed them both! He's got to pay!"

Wallace grabbed my arm. "Wait a minute."

I stiffened, terrified. Wallace had always scared me, but now I was more afraid of Mrs. Mallone and her lies about me.

"He poisoned that apple!" Mrs. Mallone pointed at me. "He was always asking questions about my remedies, about what they did. And then he used them to kill my husband. Poor Hopeful must have caught on, so he killed her too. He's got to pay for what he did. He's got to die too. Wallace, I trust you to see justice done."

Wallace told her, "He's only a boy. We can't just kill him. I'll send someone back to Independence for a sheriff. He can sort this out."

Mrs. Mallone's voice hardened. "If you won't take care of this, I know someone who will. Do you think you can keep him here for me, Wallace? Can you do that one thing right for me?" She floated haughtily away over the grass like a vengeful black swan bent on capturing its prey.

I glanced up at Wallace. "I didn't do this." My voice was a frightened croak. "I swear it. I didn't."

Wallace stared hard at me. "Then who did?"

"You won't believe me if I tell you." My eyes darted after Mrs. Mallone as she retreated.

Wallace looked too. "No."

"I said you wouldn't believe me."

He studied me, eyes narrowed. "No," he repeated, sounding less certain this time.

"Don't you remember? Hopeful tried telling you that day back in Independence. But you wouldn't listen."

Finally, he let go of my arm. "Stay with Ness. Don't let him go far. Don't you go far either." He gave me a shove toward where Ness had gone. Wallace returned to the people who'd gathered, explaining himself. I didn't wait to hear what he said, but ran after Ness.

At the creek, Ness laid Hopeful on the bank. He cupped his hands and dipped up water for her. She took in a good mouthful, then spat it out on the bank. "More," she insisted, her voice weak. Ness complied, and this time she swallowed the water. Then she laid her head down on the dirt and wept. "I was too late," she moaned. "Too late. He's dead. Oh, Daddy, no! I'm so sorry!"

Ness rubbed her back gently. He said nothing, but just let her cry.

I sat back on my heels and thought. I thought about poison and apples and Hopeful looking dead, but being alive. I thought about that old saying that appearances can deceive. "Wait," I said, "if you're not dead, maybe he's not either."

Hopeful hiccupped. "Please don't, Levi. Don't give me false hope."

"Think about it," I insisted. "She didn't stay in that wagon more than a few seconds. She might have seen him lying still and figured he was dead, same as she did you. We don't know for certain. Shouldn't we... shouldn't we find out?"

"She knows too much. If she wants him dead, he's dead. And I know she wants him dead. I've seen it, ever since we left. How she hates him. Hates that he moved us out of our house. She married him for that house, I think. She's wanted him dead a long time now. I just thought I could stop her."

"She wanted me dead too. She gave me that apple, you know—she wanted *me* to eat it. And I'm not dead. Because you got to me in time."

Hopeful tried to push herself up, but her arms trembled. Ness helped her sit up and kept one arm around her to hold her steady. She scrubbed her palms across her cheeks, wiping away tears and dirt. "Maybe. Maybe you're right. Oh, Levi, we've got to pray." She took Ness's free hand in both hers and closed her eyes. "Lord Jesus, let us not be too late. Don't let her take my Daddy from me." Then she opened her eyes. "Ness, can you help me? I don't know that I can walk yet."

"You think you have to ask?" Ness swept her up in his arms again. "Levi, you scout ahead. See if there's anyone by their wagon."

I moved cautiously out of the trees and scanned the hundred feet or so that separated us from the Mallone wagon. "I don't see anyone." Wallace must have led the people elsewhere. Maybe followed Mrs. Mallone, wherever she had gone.

"Run see. Check the wagon. We need to be sure."

I ran. Scrambled up the steps. Peered inside. No one there but the Reverend Eli, and he lay so still, I feared I must have been wrong. I prayed fervently that I hadn't been, even as I waved at Ness and Hopeful, then ducked into the wagon so no one would see me there.

Ness set Hopeful on the top step, and she crawled inside with him right after her. I shifted to one side so she could get past me.

Hopeful knelt beside her father, her cheek close to his lips. "I feel his breath!" she whispered. "He's alive! But only just."

I looked around for the medicine box. There! Under a neatly folded quilt, I saw the burnished wood gleaming at me. I shoved the quilt away and opened the lid. "There's one that cures and one that destroys. That's what she told me."

Hopeful groaned. "But she never would show me her remedies, not even let me touch her box. She hides those powerful ones. I don't know how—"

I cut her off. "I do. I saw." Quickly, I pulled out the bottle in the front and pushed my fingers down inside. The green fabric was soft, comforting, like stroking a kitten. I wiggled my fingers, trying to find a hidden button or latch, anything.

Something gave way under my index finger and the drawer popped forward the slightest bit. I pried it open and gazed inside. The vial of milky white fluid was gone. The other slender glass tube still rested in its soft green bed. It held a red liquid, rich red like blood from a fresh wound. I picked it up gingerly. "This has to be it." I peered closer at it, the beautiful richness of its color almost mesmerizing me. "What do we do with it?"

Hopeful held out an unsteady hand. "I know. I remember from when she saved the old woman next door."

I leaned over and placed the vial in her palm.

"I need a cup or a bowl. Anything."

Ness found an enameled mug and gave it to her. She added enough water to make a mouthful, then cautiously added two tiny drops of the red liquid to it. She tried lifting her father's head, but she was still too weak. I scooted closer and hoisted his shoulders up high enough that Hopeful could slide her knees under his head and hold him up that way. Then she gently put the cup to his lips and tilted it, pushing his bottom lip down with the cup so the mixture trickled into his mouth.

"Lord Jesus," Hopeful prayed, soft and steady, "bless our efforts. Bless this medicine and make it heal my daddy. Preserve his life, Jesus. Don't take him from me yet. Not like this. Lord, give him back to me."

Silently, I breathed my own prayer, but kept my eyes fastened on the Reverend Eli's face. Waiting and hoping, but almost not daring to believe this would work. I held my breath. Would he swallow? Did he need to swallow? Would he choke? Were we too late?

Hopeful's father answered all my questions with a shuddering cough. He stiffened, then relaxed. His eyes opened, and he sucked in a great lungful of air with a gasp.

"Thank you, Jesus!" Hopeful cried. "Oh, thank you, Jesus. Thank you! Thank you!" She put her hands over her face and burst into tears.

"Daughter?" rasped the Reverend Eli. "Is that you?"

"It's me, Daddy. I'm here. You're going to be all right." She clasped his hands in her own and looked up at me, tears still shining in her eyes. "And thank you, Levi."

From the end of the wagon, Ness said, "This ain't over, you know. Mrs. Mallone's bound to make a lot of trouble over this. We better make plans for what to do when she gets back."

CHAPTER TWENTY-THREE

Not much later, there I stood while Sanderson bound my wrists behind me. Nearby, men worked at digging two graves.

It had all happened sickeningly fast. The whole camp had assembled around the gravesite, along with me and my cousins and sisters. Most folks wept and moaned, making the loudest sorrowing noises I'd ever heard. Wallace had just brought over two crosses he'd made himself when *she* arrived in a swirl of black skirts, keening and wailing with an inhuman noise that slowly formed itself into a howled, "No!"

Mrs. Mallone rushed toward us, and she was not alone. With her came Sanderson, pistol in one hand, rope in the other. The wild card we had not expected. I couldn't guess why she'd gone to fetch him, what good he would be to her now that Wallace was within her grasp. I worried that Ness had not had time to explain to his father about the poison and the apples and everything else.

When they reached us, she gazed around the gathered people, proud and strong and regal. "Two graves!" she cried. "Two graves, and we all know who did this! This boy here, that we took in. That we helped. And look how he's repaid us."

Then Mrs. Mallone turned on me, her expression like a painting of someone filled with righteous anger and hatred. "He's the one." She aimed one finger straight at me, focusing everyone's attention on me. I felt shame scorch my ears and cheeks red, shame at being stared at by so many people. I always hate too much attention.

That's when Sanderson started tying my hands. He thought I'd done this. She'd convinced him of my guilt, and now she would convince the crowd too. I hadn't expected this. I was sure Ness had not either. Where was Ness, anyway? Last I'd seen him, he'd been guarding the Mallone wagon, insisting no one go in, that folks should wait to prepare the bodies for burial until Mrs. Mallone returned. But I didn't see him now.

And where was Jacob? Wouldn't anyone in the crowd stop this? Stop her? Surely I'd not really be dragged off to jail. Jail, or worse. Would they hang a boy only fourteen years old? Hang me too fast for the truth to come out, that Hopeful and the Reverend Eli were not dead after all?

My protests went unnoticed by anyone but my sisters and little cousins. All I could do was pray someone would step forward and stop this.

"Get him out of here." Mrs. Mallone ground the words between her teeth like bad-tasting medicine she didn't want to take. Her beautiful face had gone twisted and ragged. But still beautiful. She always took care to be beautiful, even in deep grief. For who could argue with the beautiful woman who obviously must have a lovely heart to match her looks. As I'd once believed.

"I said I would. Give me a minute." Sanderson knotted the rope, pulling it even tighter.

"Please," I begged him, twisting around to see him. "Please—the girl was my friend. Let me see her and her pa took care of."

Sanderson snorted. "From what I can see, you weren't no friend to her." Satisfied with his knots, he tugged on the rope, leading me away from those graves.

"It's a lie," I insisted, stumbling after him. "A mistake. I never hurt either of them."

From in front of Sanderson, Samson's deep voice said, "Let him stay." The blacksmith crossed his arms, making himself into a wall, immovable as stone. "I said you'd bring trouble, child," he rumbled.

"Now I hear that trouble, and I see it. But you didn't bring this with you. Oh, no. I know now that all the trouble we have here, we brought with us from the start."

I stared up at him. Never would I have imagined, back on that day he frightened me because I'd spooked those horses, that I would be this happy to see him. Relief washed away my embarrassment and eased my fear.

Sanderson looked confused. "Trouble? Yeah. I mean to get him out of here before he causes more."

"Not yet. Not unless Wallace says you can. He makes the rules here."

Ness arrived at last, stepping up beside Samson. He rested his hand on the pistol he wore at his side. "Won't take long. Few minutes, that's all. You can still make it back to Independence before the sheriff locks up for the night. Still get whatever reward she promised you."

Sanderson swung to face Ness square on. "I don't like what you're implying. You gonna back that up, or you want to take it back?" His free hand dropped low near his own sidearm.

Ness shook his head. "You think a gunfight during a funeral is a good idea? You think that's what she brought you here for? She promised you easy money. Take an unarmed youngster to jail. And now, you want to complicate that? If you shoot me, there's a hundred people here will see to it that you're the one trussed up and delivered to the law. And if I shoot you, then you can't collect." He smiled slowly, mockingly. "You're too smart for that, aren't you?"

"Fine." Sanderson spat on the ground. "Go on, then. Watch."

I swung back around, comforted by Samson and Ness keeping watch over me and my kin, though I still wondered where Jacob could be. I suspected Ness had told Samson the truth, or enough to make him willing to stand up for me. Thanks to them, I could see Mrs. Mallone confronted with her sins. Taken away to face justice for them.

I stood up straight, like Ivanhoe facing down his enemy on the field of honor. Or like Rebecca from that same book, trusting that the truth would set her free. Everyone would see I was innocent.

Wallace took his place between the two crosses. He raised his hands and waited until everyone quieted. "Lord Jesus, you know I'm no preacher," he began. "I lack wisdom and discernment, and I know that better now than I ever have before. I know you can give understanding to the foolish, for I've only now learned to value my son. I know you can make the blind to see, for you have opened my eyes to truth this day."

I filled with the hope that Ness had been able to

explain to him after all.

Wallace added, "I know you can make the dead rise again."

Mrs. Mallone had stayed huddled on the ground, her black dress billowed out around her like a storm cloud, face buried in her hands. But when Wallace said that about making the dead rise, she glanced up.

Wallace continued, "Lord Jesus, you stretched out your hand and made a cripple walk. You gave hearing to the deaf. You gave hope to the hopeless. You lifted your children up out of bondage time and again. And you did not hesitate to drive all the unrepentant sinners out of your temple."

For someone who professed to be no preacher, Wallace was doing some mighty good preaching.

Then Wallace stared straight at Mrs. Mallone. "Lucretia Mallone, are you a repentant sinner or an unrepentant one?"

Mrs. Mallone slowly rose. "What do you mean by this, Wallace?"

"I mean it was you who caused these two graves."

She gasped. "No! No, it was that boy!" She spun around, addressing everyone. "You all saw him! You saw him give my Hopeful that apple. He killed her for spite, for the color of her skin, for being too generous and kind." Her voice rose higher and higher as she expanded her lies. "He couldn't bear to take charity from a negro! So he killed her! And first, he killed my husband! I trusted him to dose the Reverend Eli! You know that! He did this!"

Wallace approached Mrs. Mallone again. Almost gently, he asked, "Why, Lucretia?"

"Why?" She jabbed her finger at me again. "I told you why! Haven't you heard? Haven't you seen?" She waved her hand around at those gathered. "They all saw! They all know what he did."

Wallace agreed, "They do know. They did see. They saw what *you* did."

"What I did? Why, I tried to stop her from taking that apple. I tried to save my girl! I cried out to her and I—"

From beyond the crowd, Hopeful said, "To think I used to call you Mother."

Mrs. Mallone jerked around to see where the voice came from. When she saw Hopeful walking toward us, she screamed. Not a theatrical sound this time, but a scream of real terror.

Hopeful kept coming steadily, determinedly.

Ness moved around so that his pistol could cover both Sanderson and Mrs. Mallone if need be.

Mrs. Mallone cowered away from Hopeful. "You're dead! You're a ghost!" She spun in a slow circle, eyes wild, asking everyone else, "Can you see her? Can you hear her?"

No one answered. People shifted uneasily at this

twist of events, but not one even murmured.

"I'm no ghost." Hopeful held up her stepmother's ornate hand mirror "See? I have a reflection. The mirror never lies, you said. Look! Do you see me? I'm no ghost."

Mrs. Mallone gazed at the mirror, eyes so wide I could see the whites all around her irises.

"Ghosts can't eat, can they?" Hopeful raised her other hand, a shiny red apple clenched in her fist. She took a bite, crunching loudly through the fruit's skin and flesh, her eyes locked on her stepmother. Deliberately, she chewed and swallowed. "You failed. We lived."

"No, no, no," Mrs. Mallone moaned. She closed her eyes and sank back to the ground.

Another voice spoke behind us, deep and rich and strong. "That's what I said, every time you raised that cup to my lips. I begged you, 'No. Please, no.'" The Reverend Eli came closer. "You promised if I drank it, you would spare my child. But that was another lie, wasn't it, wife?" He spat the last word, using it as an epithet.

Wallace asked again, "Why, Lucretia? Why did you do this?"

"You know why." Mrs. Mallone laughed, high and hysterical. "You *are* why. I want to be with you, love you, live in your house. Your real house, not some filthy dugout. I did it for you! I only wanted to be with you!"

Wallace's eyes widened. "We will *never* be together." He forced the words out, fists clenched at his sides. "If I'd known you thought—" He backed away. "I never dreamt—"

"Never? Oh, no, no, no." Mrs. Mallone clapped both hands over her face. Suddenly, she twisted away from all of us, running toward the road. Her skirts streamed out behind her in a black shadow. I thought for a moment they would let her get away, for everyone stood staring, too shocked to move.

Then the Reverend Eli bellowed, "Stop her!" His voice, usually rich and mellow, became a roar of righteous fury. "She must be stopped!"

Wallace reached her first, before Ness or Samson or any of the others who gave chase. He held her by the arm, dragging her back to where the rest of us waited still. No one spoke. No one even whispered. This was not our trouble to interfere in.

Mrs. Mallone fought against Wallace's grip, but his fingers closed around her arm like the talons of a hawk. Finally, he dropped her between her husband and stepdaughter.

"Stop me?" she moaned. "You can't stop me. No one can stop me now." She drew something from her skirt pocket. "I'll stop you!"

I realized one moment too late what she held. "No, don't!" I yelled, but it was no use.

Mrs. Mallone lifted the vial of gray poison to her lips and drained it. Her eyes widened unnaturally, and she stiffened, then slumped over sideways, her unseeing stare fixed on her husband.

The Reverend Eli gazed down at her, tears in his own eyes. "And so, farewell," he murmured.

CHAPTER TWENTY-FOUR

After Mrs. Mallone died, the crowd dispersed. I stayed there, hands still bound behind my back, wishing someone would untie me. My sisters and little cousins gathered around me, hugging me and rejoicing, but none of them could loosen Sanderson's knots.

That's when Jacob came running up from the road, with Hauer right behind him. They both slowed when they saw everything had already ended before they arrived.

"Jacob!" I said, loud enough to get his attention. "Jacob, where were you?"

"Fetching help." Jacob took the rope from Laura. Hauer stepped between us and Sanderson, forcing him away from me. Sanderson did not protest.

"I thought you'd left me," I told my cousin.

Jacob untied me with nimble, welcome fingers.

"Why would you think that? You can't have believed I'd do that." He slid the loops off my hands.

When I brought my hands around in front of me, my arm muscles ached more than I'd expected. I studied my wrists so I wouldn't have to look at Jacob, wincing at how much skin the rope had scraped away. "Not really, I guess. I just worried it. You disappear sometimes, is all. And I needed you here."

"I'm sorry. I'll try not to do that anymore." Jacob looked at me. Really seeing me, not half-ignoring me the way he'd done for so long. Like he'd finally remembered who I was.

I wanted him to keep remembering it. Then he wouldn't dismiss me as another little kid. I kept talking, saying anything to keep him looking at me. "Know what? I think I like Kansas."

Jacob laughed. "Even with all that's happened? Even though you almost got hauled away to jail?"

"Even so, I like Kansas." That was true. Already the land had flattened out some, not always rolling and tossing the way Missouri had. The farther we got from the river, the flatter it would be, people said. I wanted that. Missouri seemed too much like back home in Illinois. I didn't want to think about Illinois so much anymore. I wanted our new lives to begin.

Jacob reached over and ruffled my hair. "Good. 'Cause you're stuck here."

"So are you."

"So am I." He grinned. "I wouldn't mind moving along toward Junction City, though." He nodded toward the circled wagons. "Looks like everyone else is packing up too."

Sure enough, almost everyone bustled about, loading wagons, dousing cookfires, and harnessing teams. Everyone except Hopeful and Ness. They stood some distance away from all of us, talking earnestly with the Reverend Eli, who had seated himself on an upturned bucket.

Wallace approached the three of them, hat off. He turned it around and around in his hands, and he waited for them to acknowledge him before he spoke. "I've come to apologize," he said, loud enough for everyone nearby to hear. "I may not have known she... your wife... had designs on me, but that's no excuse. I ought to have seen it. I ought not to have paid her so much attention. Her being your wife... anyone's wife... I wouldn't let myself think I was doing wrong, taking notice of her that way, but I was."

"I forgive you," said the Reverend Eli. "And I understand. You see, she blinded me too."

Wallace continued, "Ness, I got no reason to hope you'll forgive me, but I'm asking just the same. Just in case."

Ness didn't use words for his answer. He grasped

Wallace's shoulder and pulled him closer, wrapping his arms around his father.

Wallace held onto Ness a moment. Then he stepped back, wiped his eyes on his sleeve, and put his hat back on. Awkwardly, he reached out a hand to Hopeful. She took it, and he placed her hand in Ness's. Wallace closed his own hands around theirs for a silent moment.

Then Wallace stepped away from them and came over to us. He asked Hauer, "You think you could take that off my hands?"

For a minute, I thought he was talking about us and our wagons. Then I saw he meant Sanderson.

Hauer sounded disgusted. "Sure will." His voice changed to kindly when he asked, "What about you Daltons? You want to tag along with my outfit until Junction City?"

Before we could answer, Wallace said, "You're welcome to stay with us, if you'd rather."

I nodded at Jacob, who said, "I think we'll do that. Hopeful could maybe use the help." He glanced at his two brothers chasing grasshoppers in the tall grass, their tears and worries for me forgotten. "Or the distraction."

Wallace said, "That's settled, then. Best get ready to move out."

"Yes, sir!" Jacob and I said together.

By the time the wagons rolled ahead onto the

road, someone had put Mrs. Mallone's body in one of the two graves and filled it in. The Reverend Eli stood beside the mound until we left, and that was all. She had no real funeral, no mourners. Everyone seemed eager to leave her behind.

Our wagon train camped for three whole days outside Junction City so we could prepare for Ness and Hopeful's wedding. No one said so, but I know we were also giving the Reverend Eli time to regain his strength. A second dose from the vial of blood-red restorative had given him the wherewithal to confront his wife, but her betrayal staggered him, and it took him some time to recover.

We'd pressed on through Kansas after her burial, watching the rolling land stretch and flatten around us. Every step of those horses and mules was a step closer to our new homes.

As I recollect, my eagerness and my nervousness increased with each passing day. Uncle Matthew was our one hope for staying together as a family, for building a new home. But we had no way of knowing how he would view us. Seems foolish now, how much I feared him, but it made sense then. He held our lives in his unseen hands.

Uncle Matthew did not meet us at Junction City when we arrived shortly after noon, hot and dusty and anxious to be done with our traveling. Ness took us to the telegraph office, and the man there assured us our telegram had been delivered. He found someone willing to ride over to our uncle's place and let him know we'd arrived. We went back to our wagons in the circle we'd formed outside town, close by the river.

I didn't think it was much of a city, not compared to Independence. Junction City didn't even have a newspaper. It did have a railroad depot and a hotel, Lutheran and Episcopal and Baptist churches, and a crowd of shops and houses. Someone told us they had two thousand people living in that town, but I think they added in all the homesteaders and farmers thereabouts. Not that we spent much time at all within the city limits. We stayed too busy getting ready for the wedding to wander around a town where nobody knew us.

Once the Reverend Eli rose from his sick bed, he was a changed man, vital and stronger every hour. Hopeful doted on him. She said she had her father back at last. I gathered she believed her stepmother had been dosing him with laudanum or worse to keep him weak and docile ever since they'd left their home behind.

I thought he'd maybe settle there and start a church in Junction City to be near Hopeful and Ness when they moved to Wallace's ranch. But some folks had already established the First Colored Baptist Church and were meeting in a school house on Sundays, so he decided to press on with the rest of his companions, still seeking their new lives in the Promised Land of Kansas.

It wasn't until the evening before the wedding that Uncle Matthew finally found us. We were sitting around our cooking fire after supper, singing songs and keeping Hopeful company on her last night as an unmarried girl. Ness sat beside her on a blanket, and he noticed Uncle Matthew first. He must have heard him arrive over the noise of our singing, for he peered into the dusk and asked, "Who's there?"

A tall man stepped in between our two wagons. Lanky and broad-shouldered, he had shaggy brown hair and a few days' growth of beard. He reminded me more of my memories of my pa than of Uncle Drew. "The name's Matthew Dalton. I believe these youngsters are looking for me."

Jacob stood. "Yes, sir, we are."

Uncle Matthew held out his hand. "You must be Jacob." He shook with Jacob, man-to-man, and then he looked down at me. "And you're Levi."

"Yes, sir."

He held his hand out to me too, just the way he had to Jacob. I jumped up and shook his hand, happy and proud that he appeared to take me as seriously as he did my cousin.

Uncle Matthew nodded at the girls and smiled at the little boys, learning their names. I don't know who acted more shy that evening, us or our uncle. He joined our circle around the fire, sitting on the other side of Jacob, but he didn't say much. He mostly watched and listened.

I found myself worrying about our life ahead with him. After all, Uncle Matthew was a stranger, really. A tall, quiet stranger. I gazed at him in the firelight, and I feared he would be a stern man, unused to the ways of youngsters.

But then Hopeful's words came back to me. *It doesn't matter what you look like so much as what you do.*

Uncle Matthew might look like a stranger. But he'd come to get us, and he promised now to take us into his home and care for us. That's what mattered.

That comforted me, and I joined in when Hopeful taught us a new song, something about waiting on the Lord and going out to the wilderness to find him. It had no end of verses, and as long as Hopeful kept supplying new ones, we sang it around and around.

I still wondered about Uncle Matthew, though. What would he think of my ambitions to be a doctor someday? Despite Mrs. Mallone's treachery, I felt the desire to heal and cure burning strong inside me.

But would my uncle approve of it? Would he say that ambition was fine and good, or would he frown and say I'd be needed to help on the farm even when I was all grown up? Would he tell me I should put such foolish notions out of my mind?

I could imagine him saying both. No matter. I was determined to follow that path, to learn all I could about saving people from disease and death. And from those who might misuse or mistreat them. I'm proud to say I've stuck to that determination all these years.

That night, Jacob and I rolled up in our blankets under the wagon where the girls and little ones slept, and Uncle Matthew spread his bedroll under the other. I didn't wake up once that whole night, for I felt safe and secure at last.

The morning of the wedding dawned cloudy, and I feared it would rain. But no, the clouds parted right before everyone assembled around the Reverend Eli, Hopeful, and Ness.

Hopeful was radiant in a simple dress of pale pink, with daisies and primroses plaited into a crown for her hair. Ness wore a new white shirt, and they both looked as pleased with each other as could be. Wallace stood to one side, solemn and proud.

The Reverend Eli said a few words about loving

and honoring God and each other, but I didn't pay much attention. Caleb had sidled over to Uncle Matthew and leaned against his leg. Uncle Matthew looked down, startled. He grabbed Caleb, swooping him up over his head to seat him on his shoulders. Caleb laughed with glee just as the Reverend Eli finished speaking, and everyone looked at him and laughed themselves, gently and kindly.

Hopeful took Ness's hand, and they jumped over a broom together, which made everyone cheer and clap, and that ended the wedding. Someone had bought a hog and butchered it, and they'd cooked it in a pit dug right in the ground, dressed with vinegar and I don't know what-all. It made for the juiciest pork I'd ever eaten. All the women had baked cakes and bread and anything else special they could find the ingredients for, and we ate ourselves almost sick.

Next morning, we made our goodbyes. Uncle Matthew said that since it would take at least two days to drive out to his homestead, we'd best get started.

Hopeful hugged us. She tucked a folded paper envelope into my shirt pocket. "Might be a place for apple trees by your uncle's house," she told me. I didn't know how to thank her for sharing some of her precious apple seeds with us, so I just hugged her one more time. I think she understood.

The Reverend Eli surprised us by laying his hands on our heads and blessing us each in turn. We climbed in our wagons, with Uncle Matthew driving one, Jacob driving the other, and the rest of us riding inside for once. With a jolt, we rolled forward into our new future.

Hopeful and Ness and Wallace and the Reverend Eli watched us, and Hopeful waved until the road curved and we could see them no more.

As I watched the road flow out behind us like a sluggish river, I pondered the changes a month could bring. Or a week. Even a day. You couldn't stop life from unspooling behind you any more than you could stop that road from stretching into the distance. You couldn't prevent life's changes from redirecting your path, with or without your say-so.

I'd learned much those few days we spent with Hopeful and Ness, Wallace and Hauer, the Reverend Eli and Mrs. Mallone. I'd learned to see the evil that lies behind believing your desires are worth more than someone else's life. I'd learned that the loveliness of a face might not be matched by lovingkindness in the heart. And I'd learned that no matter how different folks look or sound or behave, they're all the same mess of fears and hopes and wants on the inside.

DISCUSSION QUESTIONS

1. What elements of "Snow White and the Seven Dwarfs" do you recognize in *One Bad Apple*?

2. Are there any parts of the original fairy tale you wish would have been added to this story?

3. What themes can you find in this book? Are they different from the themes in the original fairy tale?

4. Who is the real hero or heroine in this book?

5. Did your opinion of any of the characters change over the course of the story?

6. Would you have liked being a pioneer? Why or why not?

7. What other stories do you know of that feature Black people in the Old West?

8. *One Bad Apple* also contains elements from William Shakespeare's play *Hamlet*. Can you spot some of them?

SUGGESTED READING

If you would like to learn more about Black pioneers, lawmen, and cowboys, I recommend these books.

FOR YOUNGER READERS:

Black Frontiers: A History of African American Heroes in the Old West by Lillian Schlissel, Aladdin Books, 2000.

Black Women of the Old West by William Loren Katz, Atheneum Books for Young Readers, 1995.

Days of the Exodusters by Corrine Wentworth, Harcourt School Publishers, 2002.

Follow Me Down to Nicodemus Town by A. LaFaye, Albert Whitman and Company, 2019.

Journey to a Promised Land by Allison Lassieur, Jolly Fish, 2019.

Wagons Wheels by Barbara Breener, Harper Collins, 1984.

FOR TEENS AND ADULTS:

African American Women of the Old West by Tricia Martineau Wagner, TwoDot, 2007.

Black Cowboys in the American West: On the Range, on the Stage, Behind the Badge edited by Bruce A. Glasrud and Michael N. Searles, University of Oklahoma Press, 2016.

Black Cowboys of the Old West: True, Sensational, and Little-Known Stories from History by Tricia Martineau Wagner, TwoDot, 2010.

Black Exodusters in Flint Hills of Kansas: Gupton-Harding Families by Karen Scroggins Campbell, Karen S./Scroggins, 2017.

The Black West: A Documentary and Pictorial History of the African American Role in the Westward Expansion of the United States by William Loren Katz, Touchstone Press, 1996.

Exodusters: Black Migration to Kansas after Reconstruction by Nell Irvin Painter, W. W. Norton and Company, 1992.

ACKNOWLEDGEMENTS

I wrote this book for the glory of God and for the benefit of my neighbor. God has given me the ability, means, and desire to tell stories, and my neighbor (that's you) gives me the reason to write them down and share them. To God alone be the glory.

My husband Larry supplies me with coffee, Coca-Cola, and the money to buy research books that I can't find through our local library. He also gives me his support and encouragement, and takes the kids on long walks now and then so I can write. My children give me hugs and kisses and the most appreciative audience an author could ask for. Thank you, all of you!

Deborah Koren is more than my best friend, more than my writing mentor, more than my chaperone through the wilderness of words. If not for her, I would have gotten lost somewhere along the line, and this story would have remained a tangled mess. Thank you! I am loving your work, cowboy.

I owe a debt of gratitude to my sensitivity readers, Lola and Tracy. Thank you for the wisdom and knowledge you both shared with me. Thank you for reading my book and answering my questions. Beggar that I am, I am even poor in thanks; but I thank you, ladies!

Erika Ohlendorf takes the essence of my books and turns them into art. Her covers are better than my words deserve. Thank you, sister!

And to my beta-readers and proofreaders, I give a thousand thanks and hugs! Olivia, Eva-Joy, Katie, Heidi, Beverly, Sam, Sadie, and Abby, you all helped me so much!

Finally, thank YOU, reader, for reading my books. Thank you for sharing them with your friends and family. Thank you for writing me to tell me what you think of them and what fairy tales you hope I retell next. You make me happy!

Turn the page to read an excerpt from book two in the Once Upon a Western series.

ONCE UPON A WESTERN · STORY TWO

DANCING & DOUGHNUTS

RACHEL KOVACINY

"Twelve Dancing Princesses" reimagined...

Fifty dollars just for asking a few questions? Jedediah Jones figures it must be his lucky day. What dancing and doughnuts have to do with anything, he neither knows nor cares. He's only interested in earning that money so he can finally eat something other than the apples he's been living off for days. Once his stomach and his pockets are filled again, he plans to move on.

But answering the advertisement plunges him into a forest of painted trees, twelve pretty sisters, trouble, and more trouble. And, yes, doughnuts. So many doughnuts.

Can Jedediah Jones solve the mystery and earn that fifty dollars when the whole town has failed? Or will the twelve sisters lose their family's business no matter what he does?

DANCING AND DOUGHNUTS

I dropped my hat on that chair full of books, put both my hands on his desk, and leaned forward. This man might have weighed the same as two of me, but I wouldn't have made sergeant major if I'd let myself be intimidated by every man who was bigger than me. Especially since I've encountered a lot of them on this earth. "How would I know that? I don't even know what you need me to do. Only a fool would say he could solve a problem he knows nothing about." I straightened and crossed my arms over my chest.

Beside me, the little lady chuckled. Or possibly she had tried delicately to restrain a cough. I didn't take my eyes off the man to find out.

He smiled, baring strong, fierce teeth. "I'm glad to know you're not a fool, at least." He held out a meaty hand. "Will Algona. I think I'm pleased to meet you, Jedediah Jones."

I shook his hand, making sure my own grip matched the firmness of his. "Glad to know you."

"Pull up a chair. That is, if you can find it."

Moving those books that filled the only other chair would have taken more time than it was worth. There must have been thirty of them. I marveled that the chair could stand up under the strain of all those words. "I'll stand, thanks."

"Then I'll be brief. Mr. Jones, someone is trying to ruin us."

"How's that?"

"They're adding liquor to the cider we serve during dances. Three times now, our girls have been rendered intoxicated. Three dances running, now."

Mrs. Algona put in, "My daughters, tipsy!"

"All those young ladies in the kitchen, they're your daughters?" I'd noted six in that kitchen, and I decided I ought to respect this tiny woman even more, if she'd borne six girls and retained such sprightly ways. My own ma only had four children, myself being the youngest, and by thirty she'd been too worn out to do much more than cook and mend and try to sweep out all the dirt we brought in the house. Though maybe six girls were easier to tend than four boys. Not having ever had sisters, I wouldn't know.

"They are," she answered. "And I take it as a personal insult that someone thinks it's funny to set them tipsy."

Will Algona said, "You act like it's a joke, Martha. It's no joke. Some wretch intends to put us out of business. They're threatening our livelihood, that's what." He shook his head. "All our plans, our hopes for the girls—and you think this is a joke. Once, that would be a joke. Maybe even twice. But three weeks running? That is pure, deliberate malice. It needs to end."

"So let me get this straight," I said. "You don't serve liquor during your dances?"

Mrs. Algona huffed. "Of course not! We serve coffee, cider, and doughnuts. We are a respectable establishment. Anyone who wants a stronger drink than apple cider has to go on over to the saloon. And if they've had more to drink than they ought, they can't come in here."

Will nodded. "That's our rules."

"No liquor—we had to practically vow on the Bible about that. We didn't exactly thrill the good folks of the town when we opened this place." Mrs. Algona sniffed. "Misunderstood our intentions, that's what they did. But they've come around."

Will said, "Plenty of people like having somewhere to come socialize after a long week of work. Old and young alike, though we do tend to mostly draw lonesome young men looking for a dance with a nice girl and something sweet to eat. If we added liquor to that mix..." He held up his hands, then let them drop to his sides. "Besides, we insist that our daughters be treated right. No drunken cowboy will get within ten feet of my daughters."

"What about the other girls who work for you? Might one of them be dissatisfied with her pay? Or angry at another girl? Maybe they quarreled about some young cowhand?"

"You don't understand," Will Algona said. "This is a family business. We don't hire anybody to work here."

"So those six young ladies I saw—"

Mrs. Algona interrupted me. "Twelve, Mr. Jones. We have twelve daughters."

I wished then that I'd set myself down when offered a chair. "Twelve?"

"Twelve," she repeated, face lighted with pride.

"I see." Twelve daughters. No wonder the Algonas wanted this sorted out soon. Twelve tipsy daughters must be right challenging to deal with....

Don't miss the first Once Upon a Western book!

"Little Red Riding Hood" re-imagined...

Mary Rose feels uneasy around Mr. Linden from the moment she meets him on the stagecoach ride to her grandmother's ranch in Wyoming Territory. But since he works for her grandmother, that means he's trust-worthy, doesn't it? Everyone else seems to view him as honest and respectable. Mary Rose wonders if she's overreacting.

She tries to ignore her suspicions until one night, she discovers his real reason for being at the ranch. Now, if she's going to save her grandmother—and herself— she's going to need to run faster than she's ever run before.

Mary Rose's adventures continue in this FREE short story, available now for Kindle, Nook, and Kobo.

"Goldilocks and the Three Bears" reimagined...

Adventurous, imaginative Mary Rose simply wants to explore a little more of the Wyoming mountains around her grandmother's ranch. She knows that once winter arrives, she'll be stuck at the ranch for months and months. She seizes her chance for one last autumn outing and heads for a beautiful lake her new friends have told her about. But a blizzard descends while she's out riding alone, trapping her in a cabin inhabited by three fierce and furry strangers.

Whether you got to know Mary Rose in her Little Red Riding Hood adventure, Cloaked, *or are meeting her for the first time, you'll find plenty of excitement in her company!*

Deputy Christopher Small and Mary Rose O'Brien have an unexpected encounter in this FREE short story, available now for Kindle, Nook, and Kobo.

"Three Billy Goats Gruff" reimagined…

Deputy Christopher Small is running out of time. He doesn't want to disappoint his little brothers by neglecting to play the annual autumn prank they're anticipating, but he needs to get himself all slicked up for dinner. Why? His parents have invited Miss Mary Rose O'Brien, the girl he's sweet on. Will he have time to do both?

Find out in this free short story that follows both the book Cloaked *and the short story "Blizzard at Three Bears Lake."*

ABOUT THE AUTHOR

Born only a few miles from where Jesse James robbed his first train, Rachel Kovaciny has loved the Old West all her life. She now lives in Virginia with her husband and their three homeschooled children. In her free time, Rachel writes a column on Old West history for the *Prairie Times*, reads, blogs, watches movies, and daydreams.

Visit rachelkovaciny.com
to sign up for Rachel Kovaciny's newsletter
and receive the exclusive FREE short story
"Let Down Your Hair."

Made in the USA
Middletown, DE
31 August 2020

16923407R00146